GUARDING PAYTON

BROTHERHOOD PROTECTORS WORLD

TEAM WOLF
BOOK FOUR

JEN TALTY

Montana D-Force (#3)

Cowboy D-Force (#4)

Montana Ranger (#5)

Montana Dog Soldier (#6)

Montana SEAL Daddy (#7)

Montana Ranger's Wedding Vow (#8)

Montana SEAL Undercover Daddy (#9)

Cape Cod SEAL Rescue (#10)

Montana SEAL Friendly Fire (#11)

Montana SEAL's Mail-Order Bride (#12)

SEAL Justice (#13)

Ranger Creed (#14)

Delta Force Rescue (#15)

Dog Days of Christmas (#16)

Montana Rescue (#17)

Montana Ranger Returns (#18)

Defending Avery - Regan Black

GUARDING PAYTON

TEAM WOLF BOOK 4

USA Today Bestselling Author
JEN TALTY

CHAPTER 1

AS A LITTLE GIRL, Payton Wheeler loved to visit her grandfather at his ranch which was located outside the small town of Cooke City, Montana, and bordered Yellowstone National Park. It had been so different from the world in which she'd been raised.

She'd grown up in New York City's Upper East Side, and while she had few complaints about her childhood, there had always been a pull toward wide-open spaces. The great outdoors.

The wilderness.

As a child, it was the adventures she'd go on with her grandfather. It was seeing the massive animals in their natural habitat.

Whenever she could, she'd spend time in Central Park with her nanny, pretending to be a cowgirl. She didn't care if it was the dead of winter or the hottest of summer days. She'd go running around the park, pretending to be a Yellowstone Ranger protecting a bear and her baby cubs.

There was something magical about an area of land that didn't have a lot of buildings or pavement on it.

Wheeler Creek Ranch had always been her happy place. But it also reminded her of the most painful decision she'd ever had to make.

And her grandfather made sure she'd never forget her choice. Not because he didn't agree or support her. He'd helped her and held her hand every step of the way. She couldn't have asked for a kinder, gentler man to be her lifesaver. But he'd also wanted that child to be a part of his life.

His legacy.

He'd felt she'd robbed him of that; though he'd never used that word, she felt it, especially the last few times she'd come to visit.

She sucked in a deep breath and pushed that thought out of her mind as she stood over the dead wolf.

A gray wolf.

An alpha.

On her property.

Her grandfather would be heartbroken. She ran her fingertips over the locket that dangled from her neck. Inside was a picture of her and Granddad taken when she'd been ten years old. Tears stung her eyes. Her grandfather had entrusted her with the thing he loved most.

His land and everything that it stood for, which included the gray wolf. He'd fought long and hard to make sure the wolf was protected. That once they'd been reintroduced to Yellowstone, the poachers and those who wanted to cause them harm were punished. He'd hate the new hunting laws and he'd be making all kinds of noise in protest of anyone who dared to hunt them. He didn't believe they were a menace. They were part of the ecosystem. They deserved their rightful place on this planet as part of the circle of life.

Hunting them for sport should be forbidden.

"The wolf was shot." Daisy Dutton lifted her cowboy hat off her head, then ran a hand across her long hair before placing her Stetson back on and adjusting it. Daisy had become one of Payton's favorite ranch hands. She was the kind of woman who didn't put up with crap from anyone. Being a cowgirl in a mainly male-dominated business had to be tough, but Daisy held her own and she had Payton's respect.

Daisy was in her late twenties, about the same age as Payton. She'd worked on the ranch since she was sixteen and Payton's grandfather considered her family; therefore, so did Payton. That's the way things were done at the Wheeler Creek Ranch.

Payton turned, facing north. The road was only

a quarter of a mile away at this point and you could see it through the trees at the bend. The property was fenced, and this area was generally used for cattle, though two days ago she'd moved them to a different pasture. She didn't think that had anything to do with this crime, but it was something to consider.

"There is no blood trail, so the wolf had to have died instantly," Daisy said. "At least I hope the poor thing didn't suffer."

"Did you hear a gunshot?" Payton asked. She wasn't sure what questions she should pose. But she needed to assess the situation before the media got wind, and they would, and she suspected they wouldn't be kind to her considering they still thought of her as an outsider.

"No," Daisy said.

"Neither did I," Colin Barnaby, the ranch's foreman, said. Colin was in early thirties and he and Daisy had just moved into the cabin on the hill together. However, they were always incredibly professional on the ranch. If a stranger saw them working side by side, they would never guess they were a couple.

Payton appreciated that.

Making friends with women hadn't been something that Payton had been able to do most of her life. She found that most of her counterparts were competitive, especially in the workforce, and that's where she'd generally met other females in the past.

But the ranch was different than the corporate world, and Montana was a far cry from New York City.

"We didn't have anyone working in this field for the last twenty-four hours," Colin said.

Even though Payton had been running the ranch for the last six months, she still didn't know all the ins and outs. She relied heavily on Colin and Daisy, as well as Topper Cohen, the ranch manager who currently paced a few feet away while his cell was pressed against his ear.

"What brought you back here?" she asked.

"I called him," Daisy said with a narrowed stare. "I'm the one who found the wolf."

"That was not meant to be accusatory." Payton pulled her ponytail over her shoulder and twisted the hair. Her nerves were fried and it came out in her tone. But also, reading women was damn impossible for Payton. "I'm just trying to figure out what happened, and you know the authorities are going to ask the same questions."

"I know." Daisy nodded. "I was riding from lot three to lot seven, checking the fence line. I noticed a break in the fence." She pointed toward the path that was often used on horseback riding excursions. "That's when I saw the wolf."

"Ma'am," Topper said. "The Yellowstone Ranger

is five minutes out." Topper had worked for her grandfather for as long as she could remember. He was about the same age as her dad and the two of them had gone to high school together. Back in the day, they had been best friends. But when her mom and dad became an item, that changed everything.

The ranch had been in the Wheeler family since the late eighteen hundreds. It was one of the few original ranches left where many of them had been sold off to make commercial properties of some kind, or worse, more houses.

The last thing Montana needed was more condominiums or another resort.

While it made sense to her that her grandfather left her the ranch, it didn't to most everyone else, including her parents.

Especially her father.

She could understand why the ranch hands didn't trust or believe she could run the operation. She hadn't ever worked there, or any place like it.

Ever.

Her experience had been limited to a few weeks every summer from the time she was an infant through her freshman year in college.

Edward Grant Wheeler had been her hero. Throughout her entire childhood, she idolized him, a big bone of contention with her father. It wasn't that she didn't love and adore her dad.

She did.

Her father, Greg Grant Wheeler, was very different from his father. They were like oil and water. Her granddad love hiking, horseback riding, fishing, and anything that had to do with the great outdoors.

Her dad enjoyed being outside, but only if he had a golf club in his hand. Or maybe a tennis racquet. Where her grandfather preferred a glass of moonshine, sitting around a campfire, and telling dirty jokes, her father would rather enjoy a three-hundred-dollar bottle of wine and eat caviar while listening to classical music and debating policy.

"Thanks for the update." Payton rubbed the back of her neck. Having a wolf die on your property was one thing.

But murdered?

Well, that was going to bring the kind of attention to her ranch that she didn't need. It was hard enough that there were those who wanted her to fail. There were people on the ranch who would have preferred she'd sold it, and that included Topper. Of course, he believed that her grandfather should have at least left a piece of it to him instead of leaving everything to a thirty-year-old girl who knew *jack shit,* to quote him, about ranching.

However, he'd sucked it up because he said he loved the ranch more than he loved the idea of owning a piece of it. He told Payton that as much as he resented her grandfather's decision, he respected his wishes. Being part of the ranch and its legacy was more important to him than owning it.

However, he made his disdain clear every time she made a decision he did not agree with.

There were two things she could count on from Topper.

His loyalty.

And his opinions.

He gave the latter a little too freely sometimes. However, he did what was necessary and he'd always been there to help her when she needed it.

Like right now.

In the last few months, there had been a half dozen or so articles about the legal and illegal hunting of wolves. It was a controversial topic, to say the least. Half the general population thought the gray wolf was a menace. The other half was grateful they'd been restored to Yellowstone and were thriving.

Her grandfather had fought tooth and nail for the gray wolf. As a young girl, she remembered how passionate he'd been, and it rubbed off on her.

"There's something you should know." Topper tucked his cell into his back pocket and planted his hands on his hips. He glanced toward the sky at the sound of blades cutting through the wind.

Payton covered her eyes and squinted. "Shit," she mumbled. "How the hell did this get out so fast?" One of the local news channels flew low over the pasture. She held up her hand when Topper opened his mouth. "It was a rhetorical question."

"Ma'am." Colin gunned the ATV, kicking up dirt. He came to a quick stop a few feet from where she stood. "We have a different problem."

"What's that?"

He nodded his head toward the path that led up to the road. "People are gathering." He blocked the view of the dead wolf. "They have phones and I'm going to assume they are filming."

"What difference does it make? If they stay on the other side of that fence, I can't ask them to leave. Besides, that chopper up there is going to put us on the evening news," she said.

"But they will at least try to get our statement as well as the wildlife agents' and the park rangers'. Those people out there are more lovers or—"

"In my case, haters." She craned her neck.

Daisy came up beside her, turning her back to the emerging crowd trying to hide in the brush. "I know it's frustrating the way many have treated you in this town, but to them, you're an outsider. They don't care that you were Eddy Wheeler's granddaughter. You weren't raised here."

"I was born here," she mumbled. "Not to mention I haven't done anything that those who fear me thought I would. I have not sold any part of the ranch to developers, and I don't plan to."

"You would think that would help your cause," Colin said. "Except between your cattle crashing the south gate and causing some problems with Yellowstone bison, and a few other minor problems, people still don't like or trust you."

"You're starting to sound like Topper." The last thing Payton needed was any more attention brought to her, but that's exactly what she was going to get. There was no way around that. However, she needed to manage the situation, cooperate with every agency that stuck their nose into the mess, and somehow come out without a scratch.

That was not going to be easy when the ten or so people standing by the fence were arguing—loudly—about whether or not the gray wolf should be hunted at all.

Wonderful.

"Go back to the city, sweetheart. You don't belong here," some guy shouted.

"Yeah. If you weren't here, I bet these murdering assholes wouldn't be killing on your property. You're weak," another one said. "Go home before something bad happens to you."

"That sounded like a threat." Colin rested his head on his weapon. "I'll go make sure they stand—"

"No," Payton said. "We do that and we look like we're flexing our muscles. We let the authorities deal with them." She waved her hand to the approaching ATV. Behind the driver's seat was a park ranger she'd met a few times.

Andrea Tavern.

The first meeting had been when the cattle mixed with the bison on Yellowstone land. Andrea was fair and reasonable, and Payton was glad for a familiar face.

However the gentleman sitting next to Andrea, Payton had no idea who he was, but she was about to find out.

"Payton." Andrea jumped from the ATV. "I can't say this is how I wanted to see you again."

"Me neither."

"This is my colleague and he's going to help with crowd control." Andrea waved him in the direction of the road. "Help the local authorities with all the private citizens."

Two more ATVs raced through the field.

One of them carried an agent from wildlife. Payton could tell because he had wildlife agent written all over his jacket and he jumped from the vehicle and adjusted his pants. "Who owns this land?"

"Are you seriously kidding me right now, Rob?" Andrea shook her head. "You know exactly who owns the Wheeler Creek Ranch."

"Eddy died," Rob said with a touch of sarcasm.

"Thought the out-of-towner would have listed it by now."

Shit. An agent who didn't like her and he hadn't even met her. That wasn't going to help her much.

But Andrea started off that way and she'd been warming up to Payton. Although, Andrea hadn't been that vocal out of the gate. She had the decency to keep her negative opinions to herself to begin with.

"I'm Payton Wheeler. Eddy's granddaughter and the owner." She stretched out her arm.

Rob glanced at her hand for a moment before taking it in a firm handshake. "I'd appreciate it if you and your employees moved away from the murdered creature. I worry that this is already a compromised site."

"Are you kidding? We've known each other since I was knee-high to a grasshopper." Daisy pointed to the center of her chest. "I'm the one who found the gray wolf. You know my stance on hunting them, so don't you go and accuse me of tampering with anything."

"I'd like to check out the scene with one of the deputy sheriffs." Rob waved over one of the uniformed policemen. "Let me do my job."

Payton climbed into the ATV with Colin. Daisy scooted into the back seat with Topper.

Colin eased the vehicle to the far end of the

open area, where they could watch Rob, Andrea, and the police officer survey the situation.

But they were also out of the main focus of the few people who had gathered on the road.

"Don't you think it's odd that we have such a large audience?" Payton asked to no one in particular. "I get once we called the authorities, the news crew would show up. But how did these people know? It's not like this is a well-traveled road."

"But it's not untraveled," Topper said. "Between your ranch and town, it's the main one."

"But she's got a point and it is concerning." Colin slipped from behind the steering wheel. Daisy joined him.

"I warned your grandfather that leaving this ranch to you could be dangerous," Topper said. "So far all that has happened has been a flat tire on your truck, a few nasty emails, and egg on the window. But murdering a gray wolf on your property could get you killed."

"You think this was done on purpose to run me out of town?" she asked.

"I'd say that's a good guess," Topper said.

"I agree with Topper. This could easily be someone who wants you out." Colin turned and caught her gaze. "I know an organization called the Brotherhood Protectors. They work out of West Yellowstone and have broken up some poaching rings lately."

"I've heard of them," Topper said. "They've worked with rangers and wildlife as well as the livestock commission. What do you think they can do for us? For Payton?"

"Protect her, for starters," Daisy said. "She lives in that big house all by herself and those emails weren't all that tame. One did warn her to get out of town, or else. This feels like the *or else* kind of scenario."

"You want to hire me a bodyguard?" Payton had to admit, she'd been spooked. So much so that she'd been practicing her shooting.

She wasn't that great of a shot.

A bodyguard might make sense, but it felt a bit over the top, especially when she had a bunch of muscular ranch hands living in the bunkhouse.

"They will do more than that," Colin said. "They will investigate and help figure out who is behind all this."

"But what if that dead wolf was an accident and whoever killed it is only concerned about the consequences? Not sending a message to me."

"Then we'll send the bodyguard home," Colin said. "Let me make the phone call."

She opened her mouth, but snapped it shut when the wildlife agent and Andrea strolled in her direction.

"Do you own a hunting rifle?" Rob asked as he

looped his fingers in his belt. His frosty breath hung in the cold air like thick smoke.

"I do," she said.

"When was the last time you shot it?" Rob asked.

"You don't have to answer that," Andrea said. "At least not without a lawyer present."

"We're going to ask that you go down to the station and make a statement. We're also going to ask that you take a gun powder residue test," Rob said.

"I fired my rifle yesterday and my handgun this morning." Payton avoided Topper's glare. She knew she'd fail the residue test. She didn't need a lawyer for that one.

"Why?" Rob asked. "Did you go hunting?"

Payton grinded her teeth. "No," she managed. "It was target practice."

"Well, let's hope for your sake that the bullet we pull out of that wolf doesn't match the shell casings of your rifle because even though its lawful to hunt wolves, that one is tagged. It's an alpha wolf from Yellowstone National Park. It won't matter if you have a license to kill a wolf. Alphas are off-limits. Especially tagged ones."

It's impossible to see the tag from a distance, but Payton wasn't about to remind Rob of that juicy little piece of information.

Rob shifted his stance. "If memory serves me

correctly, your grandfather never allowed wolf snaring, trapping, or hunting. I don't see any posted signs granting such permission."

"Because there is none," Payton said. "I wouldn't allow it. I'm against the hunting of wolves."

"I wouldn't say that too loudly," Rob said. "It doesn't matter what side of the fence you sit on. Once one dies either on your property or by your hands, you've got a target on your back by one of the groups. In your case, it looks like both right now."

"Colin," Payton said. "Make that phone call."

CHAPTER 2

Justice Kane sat in the common room and stared out the picture window at the mountains in the distance. He'd been all over the world and grew up in what he thought had been a small piece of heaven.

Lake Placid, New York, was still one of his favorite places on earth, but Yellowstone was a close second.

Both places had similar features.

Tall mountains.

Though Yellowstone's peaks were higher.

They both had incredible views. Great wildlife. And a blanket of stars that he loved to stare at in the evening hours while his restless heart needed some clarity.

It appeared only these two locations could offer such a calming effect on his soul.

"And then there were only two left." His long-time buddy, Wade Fielding, handed him a beer. He copped a squat on one of the wingback chairs and rested his feet on the coffee table, crossing his ankles. Wade was his best friend. His true brother, even though they weren't blood related.

"It started with just us two." Justice had known Wade since grade school. If it hadn't been for Wade and his family, Justice would have most likely ended up in jail before his eighteenth birthday. When everyone else had either let Justice down or abandoned him, Wade stood by his side.

And vice versa.

No matter what happened, Wade had always been there for Justice, even when Justice tried to pull away. Or hide. Wade had shown Justice what true friendship—what family—really meant.

"As much as I enjoy our team, I don't mind the quiet of this," Wade said.

"Do you remember the day we joined the Army?" Justice took a long sip. The cold brew tickled his throat. He'd been tripping down memory lane for hours. It wasn't just because another one of their team members had found true love and moved out, leaving Wade and Justice as the *last men standing.* But more because Justice felt as though his life had come full circle. He'd started this journey with Wade and it felt fitting to end it.

Though it wasn't ending. This was actually a new beginning for both of them.

However, things were different now that they weren't in the Army anymore.

"Your old man kicked the shit out of you for the last time." Wade reached out and squeezed Justice's shoulder.

The two men had been through a lot together. No one knew Justice the way Wade did.

No one.

Not a single person understood Justice's pain. His heartache. His scars.

"Waiting for boot camp had to be the longest few months of my life." Justice had spent the majority of his high school days at Wade's house. Every day after school. Every weekend. Basically, every chance he got. "It's funny, the last time I saw my dad, he looked like he'd aged a hundred years and I felt sad at how scared I'd once been of him."

"He'd been using you as a punching bag since you were in middle school."

"Dude, he started hitting me before that."

Wade sighed. "I hate that for you."

"It was a long time ago," Justice said. "It's hard to believe all we've been through together and now you're going to up and leave me for a woman."

"Seriously, stop with that." Wade set his beer on the table. "I'm not going anywhere."

Justice laughed. "Everyone on our team except us has a woman in their lives. You're next."

"Even if I did have a girlfriend, I'm not leaving my wingman."

"Okay. Maverick." Justice laughed. "But I want you to know that if you did, I release you of your vows to me."

"This is why I don't have a lady in my life. Everyone believes you and I are an item."

Justice raised his beer. "You are my work husband."

"The emphasis on that statement, dude, is work." Wade punched Justice in the arm. "It's going to be weird around here without Ridge."

"Let's face it. He had one foot out the door ever since we got here and he met Eris." Of all the team members, Ridge had been the hardest for Justice to get to know and it had always bothered him. Edge preferred dogs to humans, but he and Justice had bonded over the years because of their love for the four-legged creatures. They were tight. Not quite like him and Wade, but close. Same with Gabe, though that relationship was different. However, Ridge and Justice had always kept each other at arm's length. Not on the job. There, they had each other's backs like there was no tomorrow. Just not the emotional stuff. "In all the years I've worked with Ridge, these last few months were the closest we ever got. I had no idea how funny he is and I'm going to miss the man."

"Just because the love bug has a hold of him doesn't mean that will change," Wade said. He was the only one on the team who Justice could speak openly to when it came to his true feelings of abandonment. He knew he was a grown-ass man. Thirty-four to be exact. He had no reason to be concerned about whether or not any of his team would remain in his life.

He knew that wouldn't change. Even if the makeup of the team did, their relationships wouldn't. They'd been through too much together; they left the Army as a group, and they came to Yellowstone as a group.

That says a lot.

But that didn't change how difficult it was for Justice to remove his emotions from places they didn't belong.

"Look at Gabe and Edge. They are the same men."

"I wouldn't go that far." But Justice didn't begrudge them their happiness. He could see it in their eyes how much making this move to Yellowstone and finding true love had done for his brothers-in-arms. "But same isn't always what's best."

"Aw, look at you, grasshopper. You're growing up," Wade said. "But you know, cupid might find you next."

"Nope. That's never going to happen." When people heard Justice's life story, they assumed he didn't want to get married and have kids out of fear that he might be just like his father.

Well, fuck that.

He knew he was twice the man his dad could ever be. He'd never once been concerned that he was like his father. He knew his core self and he was a good person.

But he didn't trust women.

And with good reason.

His mother didn't just run out on his dad. She ran out on Justice, leaving him with a monster. He'd never understood why. When he asked his father, he told Justice flat out that she didn't want to be *his* mother. Justice didn't believe that, but then he went looking for her right before he joined the Army. One of the worst moments in his life had been when he'd found his mom.

Alive and well and living in Saratoga Springs, New York.

And remarried to a wealthy man who had two kids, making her a stepmother. It always bugged Justice that his mother would raise someone else's children, but not her own.

When confronted, she looked Justice square in the eye and told him to brace himself for his first real dose of reality.

She told him she didn't want anything to do with him or his father. That she didn't love either of them. Simple. That was that. She'd left and didn't want to look back and asked that he never contact her again.

He never would.

He accepted his mother's choices, but it hardened him in a way he didn't think he'd ever be able to bounce back from. So far, he hadn't when it came to women and romance.

Every relationship he tried to have with a woman showed time and again that he couldn't trust enough—or give enough of his heart—to go the distance.

If he couldn't do that, then he had no business being a husband or a father. It wasn't fair to whomever he dated. In all reality, it wasn't their fault. They weren't his mother. But he still couldn't see past her transgressions.

That was his reality.

So, single he would remain.

"What do you want to do tonight?" Wade asked. "I noticed a new series dropped on Netflix yesterday."

"I could be down for that."

The sound of the lobby doors opening caught Justice's attention. He glanced over his shoulder.

Stone Phillips meandered into the room. "Good afternoon, gentlemen."

"Stone," Justice said, raising his beer. "What brings you by?"

"I've got an assignment," Stone said, tucking a folder under his arm.

"For which one of us?" Wade asked.

"Justice," Stone said.

"Me?" Justice set his beverage on the counter and sat up taller. "What's the case?"

"An alpha gray wolf has been found shot on a property outside of Cooke City, Montana." Stone made himself comfortable on the small sofa in front of the window.

"Isn't that on the northern border of Yellowstone?" Wade asked.

"It is." Stone nodded. "Anyway. It was found on the Wheeler Creek Ranch and the woman who owns the ranch is considered an outsider, even though she inherited the property from her granddad. Not only is she the prime suspect in the shooting of the wolf, but according to her foreman and ranch manager, she was being harassed before the wolf was killed. He believes the two are linked and he's concerned for her safety."

"I take it you've looked at the file," Justice said. "And believe she's not guilty, or why would we be taking the case."

"There is some damning evidence, but not enough to arrest." Stone held up his hand. "Not yet anyway. I knew her grandfather. He was a good man. I've met her a few times over the years and she's a sweet young woman. She might be in over her head since the old coot left her his ranch, but that doesn't mean she should pack up and go back to New York City, which is the feedback she's getting from some of her neighbors." He handed a file to Justice. "Both Hank, Gabe, and I looked this over, and we don't like some of the things that have happened to her before the dead wolf."

"This happened today." Justice rubbed his temple as he flipped a page. There wasn't much. A few incidents that indicated some might feel threatened by her presence or that she didn't belong. "It says here that her foreman called. A guy by the name of Colin Barnaby. Does she not want protection?"

"I know Colin personally; that's why he made the call." Stone stood. "You leave as soon as you can pack your rucksack. You'll be staying on the ranch. I believe in the barn, if you're lucky."

"That's where he belongs," Wade said.

Justice laughed. It wouldn't be the first time he'd slept in a barn, but the last time he'd been a kid and had been hiding from his father after a beating. It had been when he'd come clean to Wade's parents about what had been going on, right after his sixteenth birthday. Wade's parents had suspected but didn't know for sure. A lot of people were cautious when it came to Wade and his dad. Most people just didn't want to piss off his old man out of fear for what he might do. Justice understood that fear. He lived it day in and day out.

Telling Wade's dad had been one of the hardest things he'd ever had to do. The shame had been unbearable.

But no one in Wade's family saw it that way.

Ever.

They never looked at him differently. They didn't shame him or even pity him. They simply loved him.

"You call this guy first if you need backup," Stone said, pointing a finger to Wade, as if Justice would ever call anyone else.

"Yes, sir." Justice hopped to his feet.

"Hurry home, honey. I don't like being here by myself." Wade fanned his face. "You work too much and I feel so misunderstood."

"Behave yourself while I'm gone." Justice slapped his buddy's shoulder.

"Call if you need me."

"You know I will." This would be the first solo assignment Justice had taken with the Brother-hood. His heart thumped in the center of his chest much like the first time he'd flown a helicopter by himself.

It was both a good feeling, and a bit scary.

But he knew he was right where he belonged.

CHAPTER 3

Justice turned off the lights and the engine of his pickup. He slipped from behind the steering wheel and stared at the big two-story log cabin house.

More like a mini mansion.

It was kind of funny that it was made of logs. Or at least it was to Justice.

It glowed under the moonlight with all the well-placed lights in the landscaping. It was almost too much. It nearly took away from the stars and the moon as they danced in the sky. Justice preferred that lighting to anything manmade.

Directly across from the structure stood a barn and corral. Off to the right and in the distance was another barn and a bigger corral.

And to the left was a large bunkhouse.

He only knew it was called that because he'd seen three of them since he'd moved to Yellowstone. In Lake Placid, they might be called servants' quarters. Or a guesthouse. Or he had no fucking clue. He didn't think places like this existed where he came from. At least not on this grand scale.

He reached into the back of his truck and pulled out his rucksack.

A bright light momentarily blinded him. He covered his eyes and glanced to the porch as a silhouette slinked down the stairs. "Hello? The name's Justice Wade. I'm with the Brotherhood Protectors."

"Welcome," a sweet-as-honey voice rang out. It coated his ears like chocolate melting over ice cream. The brightness dimmed and his eyes quickly adjusted. "Sorry about that. I have them set higher than normal because of what happened with the gray wolf."

"Are you Payton?"

"In the flesh." Her long dark hair flowed over her shoulders. She wore jeans, a flannel shirt, and cowboy boots. If he had to guess, she might be five foot five at best.

He swallowed his pulse. There was something stunning about the way she took the stairs one step at a time. It wasn't that she was as graceful as a ballerina, but more that she had a sense of confidence, but no one could call it arrogance.

She smiled.

And his knees buckled.

He'd seen beautiful women before and they did nothing to his ability to think or breathe. But this girl made his thoughts jumble into a puzzle that he couldn't solve.

"Thank you for coming. Are you hungry?" she asked.

"Honestly, I am. Silly me for thinking there might be a fast-food joint on the way, so when I stopped and filled my tank, I didn't bother to get a snack." Wade would be busting at the seams and at the same time, he'd be waggling his shameful finger because Justice not only wasn't all that hungry, but he had a thing of trail mix in his rucksack and he'd eaten before he left, so basically, he'd just lied.

She laughed. It was the sweetest thing that he'd ever had the pleasure of listening to.

"But really, a bag of chips and some water would be fine. I know it's getting late and you can show me to my quarters, and then I'd like to walk the grounds." He did his best to remain professional. This was his first official solo assignment. He didn't need to go and fuck it up by pathetically hitting on the client and crashing and burning.

"I was going to have you stay in the bunkhouse with the cowboys, but my foreman thought you'd be more comfortable in the house and he thought I'd be safer."

"That would be Colin, right? He's friends with Stone."

"I believe so." She waved him up on the porch.

He inched closer. He wasn't sure how he felt about staying in the main house. Granted, the safety issue was correct. He'd be able to keep a better eye on her, but he was confident in his ability to protect her from the barn—or the bunkhouse. "All I need is a place to rest my head." Staying with her would make protecting her easier. But he wasn't going to be sleeping much and that might make it hard on her in some ways. "I don't want to disrupt you or your daily routine, and I will be getting up in the middle of the night and making rounds and—"

"I've had insomnia since all this started, so you won't bother me. Besides, both Colin and Topper, my ranch manager, along with my lead cowgirl are all insisting that you should be staying in the house."

"Where are they?"

"Topper has gone home for the day." She pointed northeast. "He and his wife live in town. Daisy and Colin live in separate quarters on the property. The rest live in the bunkhouse."

"How many people do you have working for you?" He tossed his rucksack over his shoulder and followed her up the steps, doing his best not to stare at the swaying hips in front of him. She gathered her thick, wavy hair and tugged it into a messy bun at the top of her head.

He really needed to get out more. Ever since he'd moved to Yellowstone, he'd shied away from dating more so than usual. He'd always been clunky around the opposite sex. He didn't have any great moves or pickup lines. One girl he dated for a few months told him if she had waited for him to approach her, she would probably still be waiting.

That had made him laugh, but at the same time, it was sadly true. What had been worse about that situation was that out of all the women he'd gone out with, he'd cared for her the most.

But not enough to make a real thing of it.

And she'd moved on because he couldn't commit.

That had been three years ago. She'd since married two years ago and had a one-year-old. He was truly happy for her.

"I have fifteen full-time employees."

"That seems small for a ranch this size." He set his bag down by the front door and glanced up at the split staircase. The rustic two-story foyer, more like a room than an entryway, was equipped with a small reclining chair, table, reading lamp, and stack of books. He couldn't help but notice a reading device. "Do you sit there and read?"

"I do," she said. "My family room is this massive thing and I feel lost. Besides, the fireplace is right in the middle of a massive wall of windows facing the woods. With all that is going on, I feel like if someone is out there watching me or some weird shit, I'm giving them an easy target."

There had been little Justice had learned from his father; however, his dad did have a decent reputation as a contractor. He showed up. He did the job, and most of his customers were satisfied.

It was his employees who had problems with him and the way he did business.

Or the way he treated his family.

Justice did have a few handyman-type skills he'd picked up from his dad along with having more than a basic understanding of different products.

The front windows had a green hue to them and when looking out, he saw himself in the reflection.

That meant there was a privacy tint.

And the windows were new in the last five years.

"How big is this place?" he asked, making mental notes of the layout. For an older building, it had an open floor plan. He suspected the entire house had been redone when the windows had been replaced.

"It's about nine thousand square feet."

To the right of the staircase, he noticed a closed door.

To the left was a door that led to the kitchen. Off that was a dining area and the living area.

She wasn't lying when she said it was huge.

She paused by the kitchen. "The master suite is on the first floor along with a den and an office. And then there are five guest bedrooms upstairs."

"How often do you go upstairs?"

"Almost never." She laughed. "Would you like a drink? I'm going to have some bourbon."

"Sounds good to me. On the rocks, please."

"Why don't you pour it and I'll go heat you up some pulled pork."

"That sounds even better." As if on cue, his stomach gurgled.

He made his way to the bar area, which was on the far wall across from the fireplace and under the stairs, tucked in nice and neat between the split. He found a very expensive bottle of bourbon. He eyed about four fingers in each glass before strolling over to the windows. He set her glass down and stared out into the darkness.

They were definitely tinted for privacy. The only questions were how much someone could see inside and what did that backyard look like. "How many acres do you have?"

"Almost a thousand."

"That's big." He lifted the drink to his lips. He was used to cheap bourbon. The kind that burned on the way down.

This was as smooth as butter. It sailed down his

throat. He didn't cough. He didn't even flinch. He simply swallowed.

He was definitely going to have more.

"It's a decent-sized ranch." She set down a tray on the coffee table with a pork sandwich and an ear of corn. "Big, actually."

"That smells amazing."

"Enjoy." She plopped down on the sofa and sighed.

"Since you're awake, do you mind if we go over some things?" He adjusted his jeans and made himself comfortable on the dark leather sofa. "I didn't get a chance to go over all the details and my boss sent me the police report, but I was driving."

He tried to notice every detail of the ranch. The decor could only be described as masculine and rustic. It wasn't overstated, but it was something that would be noted inside a local magazine, and he had to be honest, he could get used to a place like this.

But on a much smaller scale.

At least living alone. He couldn't imagine rattling around a house like this by himself. It was the kind of home that needed a couple of kids and a family dog.

Maybe two.

He could also see a few cats, not that anyone could describe him as a cat lover. But he never said he didn't like the creatures.

"What do you need to know?" Payton asked.

"They didn't arrest you. Why?"

She tilted her head and glared.

He nearly dropped the sandwich in his lap. "I didn't mean that the way it sounded. I want to know what they told you. If you felt like they were gunning for you. If there was anyone you thought was on your side. Or wasn't on your side."

"I'll start with those I sort of trust. The Yellowstone park ranger, Andrea Tavern, doesn't believe I had anything to do with it. Or at least she was constantly defending me. The wildlife agent, Rob Altos, on the other hand, seems to have a hard-on for me and not in a good way."

Justice coughed. "Had you had issues with him before?"

"I never met him until today," she said. "But there are a lot of people who would prefer me to go back to New York and I think he's one of them."

"I'm originally from Lake Placid."

"I grew up on the Upper East Side of Manhattan and while I've been as far north as Saratoga, I've never been there."

"Not quite as magnificent as Yellowstone, but it has a lot to enjoy, like the Olympic Center," he said. "How vocal have people been about their distaste for your presence?"

"Depends on who you're talking about. I had three ranch hands quit within a month of my arrival. They flat-out told me it was me or them." She shrugged. "A couple of neighbors were afraid I was going to sell my grandfather's ranch and are still holding their breath."

"But that's all the more reason to keep you or buy it themselves if you do choose to sell." Justice scarfed down the last of his sandwich, realizing he was hungrier than he thought, and leaned back. "I glanced at some of the anonymous emails suggesting you don't belong and should go home." None of those messages came out and specifically stated what they intended to do to her. They did use the language *or else* and the tone wasn't pleasant either. "What have the authorities done about those?"

"They took the report. And they come out each time I've had an incident."

"Someone egged your house and put a nice slash in all of your tires, but the police reports note that the initial thought of the officer is that it was one of those employees who left."

"One of them was overheard trash-talking me in a bar in West Yellowstone, so yeah. The cops thought it could be them."

"What do you think about that statement?"

"It's possible, but I've thought a lot about that, and I don't understand what purpose that would serve those ex-ranch hands. They weren't fired. They quit because they had this preconceived notion that I would ruin the ranch. Well, two of them. One of them I think just didn't like the idea that he'd be working for a woman half his age. But I don't see any of them killing a protected gray wolf."

"Not even if the idea was to set you up to go down for hunting without a license? That could get you jail time."

She raised her beverage and took a sip. "What would be my motive to kill a wolf in the first place?"

"It was attacking your cattle."

"There was nothing in the field," she said. "And I can protect myself and my livestock from a wolf, if I had to. If that was the case, I'd do it. I might not have grown up here, but my grandfather made sure I understood the mentality. My only mistake was not to follow my heart when I was eighteen."

"What do you mean?" Justice asked.

"Moving out here and working with my grandpa."

"What did you do instead?"

"What most little girls do."

There was a long pause, and he wasn't sure if he was supposed to understand what she meant by that or if he was supposed to respond. "I'm not a girl, nor have I ever been one, so please, enlighten me."

"You're cute." She lifted her glass with her pinky raised.

He remembered being a young lad, before his mother left, and she'd tell him that anytime a woman drank like that, it was a sign of class and money. When he found out how she lived years later, she raised that pinky like a badge of honor. Something told him that Payton did that simply out of habit, not necessity or some weird concept that the way a woman sipped an adult beverage commanded respect.

"I was being serious. I don't know what you meant by that."

"Oh. Shit." She sat up taller. "Okay. Basically, I wanted to please Daddy. And he thought I should go to business school and if I still wanted to come out here, then maybe after I got a master's degree, but that didn't happen. I went right to work in my dad's office. I wanted his approval. You don't have to be a girl to understand that. Didn't you want yours?"

"Nope." Crap. He'd said that too quickly. For years, he'd been so ashamed of his past. Of where he'd come from, that whenever anyone asked, if Wade were around, they'd often joke about being twins separated at birth.

"You don't get along with your father?" she asked.

Not only did he open that can of worms, but Stone had mentioned that sometimes giving a little peek into his personal life would help the clients feel comfortable.

But he'd have to tread lightly into this territory and not dive right into the deep end. He needed her to trust him so she'd open up about everyone and everything.

"My dad wasn't and probably still isn't a nice man."

"May I ask when the last time was that you saw him?"

"When I joined the 10th Mountain Division at Fort Drum, it brought me pretty close to my hometown," Justice said. "When I retired with my entire team, we did many search and rescue missions in and around Lake Placid. I ran into him once or twice."

She arched a brow. "So, what you're saying is you have no relationship with him?"

"Not since I graduated from high school. To be honest, it's for the best because for years, I put up with his fist being his only form of communication. I can't trust that I wouldn't return the favor." Justice lifted the bourbon to his lips and tossed his head back. The ice cubes rattled in the glass.

So much for keeping things cool.

He had no idea why he let her in, but he had and he couldn't put that juicy tidbit back in the box. Wade always told him that sharing what had happened didn't have to be such a big emotional share, but sometimes the way Justice did it put people at arm's length.

"I'm sorry that you went through that," she said softly.

"I can't complain at this point in my life. It got me to the Army and I wouldn't change that for anything," he said. "Tell me about your parents. Are they still in Manhattan?"

"As a matter of fact, they are."

"Why didn't your grandfather leave the ranch to them?" Justice asked. "And how do they feel about you living out here and running this place?"

"My father is a little more supportive than my mom. This was his father's ranch, but he felt stifled growing up here. Isolated. He's a city man with big city dreams."

"What does he do?"

"He owns a real estate development company."

"And you used to work for him?"

She nodded.

Justice arched a brow. "I can see why some of your neighbors might be nervous about you and your plans for the ranch."

"My father and his dad didn't see eye to eye when it came to Wheeler Creek Ranch, but they respected each other. My dad supports my decision. He's supportive of me. My mom isn't as thrilled by the move. Her family is from downstate and she was born with a silver spoon in her mouth.

She doesn't think I should have to work this hard—or at all. But her biggest problem is she doesn't believe I'll find a decent husband out here so I can give her grandbabies."

"Are you looking for one? A husband that is."

"Does it matter to the case?"

"I don't know." It probably had nothing to do with anything, but he was there for a reason. No one hired the Brotherhood Protectors because they were minimally concerned. No. They were brought in because real, imminent danger was around the corner.

Something was brewing and it was his job to find it and eliminate it.

And he was damn fucking good at his job.

"My job isn't to just stand around and protect you. I'm here to help find out what is going on so that nothing else happens. I'm going to be suspicious of everyone, including your best friend. Who is that by the way?"

"I don't have one."

"Everyone has friends. So, tell me who you're the closest to."

"If I have to pick one, I'd have to say my lead ranch hand, Daisy Dutton, but I haven't made a lot of close friends out here. And sadly, the longer I stay, the more I withdraw because I don't trust that someone doesn't have it out for me."

"That's fair," he said. "Would you be willing to

make me a list of everyone who works here, ranking where you think they fall on your suspicion radar. Then do the same for people you do business with. Neighbors. And anyone else you can think of."

"I've already started one," she said. "I was told that you want to tour the property as well, so we can do that first thing."

"Good." He stood. "Would you mind showing me my quarters?"

"You can take any room on the second story."

"If it's okay with you, I'd rather stay on the first floor. Just in case something happens, I'll be ready."

"You can stay in the den. There is a Murphy bed in there and a desk if you need it, but you'll have to use the bathroom in the hallway. It doesn't have its own."

"That's fine. Of course, I'm happy to stay in the—"

"I'm not putting you in the barn. That's silly. And you really don't want to stay in the bunkhouse." She rose. "One thing that Topper is concerned about is me going to jail for something I didn't do. It's not a long sentence, but he's worried they will make an example out of me."

"That's possible. But that wouldn't necessarily get rid of you. If this is an attempt to force you to leave, this is one escalation. But you can run a business from behind bars. However, we can talk like this all night. I need a list of all the players, even people who you believe would never hurt you, so I can look at all angles."

"I'll get you as much as I can by breakfast."

"I appreciate that."

"Let me show you to the den."

He followed her back toward the foyer and to the room to the right of the stairs. Only it wasn't a room. It was a door to a hallway.

"The bathroom is the second door on the left. My office is first one. I'll try not to wake you if I end up in there before you wake up." She pointed to another door at the end of the hallway. "That goes to the master. If you need me, you can text me or knock. I'm a light sleeper, but I'll warn you. I'm so spooked, I sleep with a gun."

"So do I," he said with a chuckle. "I'll see you in the morning."

"Sleep well, Justice Kane."

He curled his fingers around the doorknob to his room while he shamelessly stared at the sexy woman clicking her cowgirl boots down the hard-wood floors toward her bedroom.

Visions of her naked between the sheets tormented his mind.

He quickly pushed those thoughts from his mind. He was there to do a job.

Not the girl.

CHAPTER 4

Pᴀʏᴛᴏɴ ᴡᴀᴛᴄʜᴇᴅ as Davey brushed down one of the show horses his father had been training. Davey had recently turned fourteen and Payton couldn't believe how tall the young boy had grown in the last few months. His voice had started to change as well.

He was turning into a fine young man, and it warmed her heart because it reminded her that she'd made the right decision.

Every time she looked at him, she saw her past. She'd been eighteen. A senior in high school.

Way too young to be a parent.

But she'd waited too long and by the time she'd come out to visit her grandfather that summer, she'd been seven months pregnant. It was amazing she'd been able to hide it from her parents. Though they'd teased her she'd put on the freshman fifteen early.

Shortly after she arrived at Wheeler Creek Ranch, she broke down and told her grandfather everything. Although, he hadn't given her much of a choice. Normally, she'd come to the ranch and be prepared to work her ass off. But not that summer. No. she'd been withdrawn and spent most of her time in her room, crying. When her grandfather confronted her, she had no idea what to do and she tried to come up with a lie, but couldn't form a decent one, so she'd blurted out her predicament.

Her grandpa took her into his arms and told her it would be okay. He didn't shame her or condemn her indiscretion.

He simply showed her kindness and love.

From there, she went to stay with an old friend of her grandpa's in Utah where she gave birth. Her grandfather arranged for a private adoption to a family who were desperate to be parents. She didn't make the connection that Davey was her son until her grandfather had died.

She was grateful Davey had no idea who she really was or that he'd even been adopted. She hoped that secret would remain buried forever. It wasn't about her, but about the boy.

And his parents.

She wondered if Charlie and Tara knew that

Payton was Davey's birth mother. She suspected not based on the way they treated Payton. They often invited her and her grandfather, before he passed, over for dinner. He would decline, stating she didn't come to visit very often and he wanted to be selfish.

Now she understood it was something entirely different.

Davey glanced up. He smiled, set down the brush, and strolled in her direction. In the last year he'd begun working more at the ranch with his father. He was always so polite and poised. He acted more like an adult than most grown men. A characteristic she attributed to his father.

The one who raised him. Not his biological one.

"Good morning, Miss Payton," Davey said. "Are you going riding this morning?"

"No. I was just looking for the man I told you about yesterday—Justice. He's staying up at the house."

"I haven't seen him," Davey said. "I'm sorry about what happened with the gray wolf."

"So am I." She looked toward the bunkhouse and then across the property toward the open fields.

No sign of Justice.

"Where are your parents?" she asked.

"My dad's in the barn." Davey jerked his head. "Mom's doing the breakfast at the restaurant. We're short-staffed. She's not happy about it either."

Payton laughed. Tara and Charlie inherited the business from Charlie's family and it brought in a decent penny for them. It also—for the most part—ran itself, so they didn't have to work there. Not to mention Charlie's brother and sister helped out as well and were part owners.

But occasionally, both Tara and Charlie were forced to show their face.

"I'm just glad she's not making me work there after I finish up here."

"Don't you have school?"

"There's some teacher thing going today and tomorrow. So, long weekend." He smiled bright. "And that new Marvel movie comes out tomorrow, so my dad said we could go. I'm super excited about that."

"Sounds like fun," she said. "I love movie theatre popcorn. It's my favorite."

"Oh. I know. It's the best." He nodded. "Well, I better get back to work. My dad doesn't like it when I pause to chat, even when it's with the boss."

"Okay. But if you see Justice, could you tell him I'm looking for him?"

"Sure thing." Davey turned on his heel and strode back toward the horse he'd been brushing.

She stared for a few long moments, knowing she'd made the right decision. The only decision for Davey.

And for herself.

She hadn't been selfish like she figured some people might call her. It had been the least selfish act she'd ever done in her life and she'd do whatever it took to protect the child.

"DADDY. I'm fine. You don't need to hop on a plane and come here." Payton sat at the island in the center of the kitchen, fiddling with her bagel and cream cheese.

The breakfast of champions, as her mother called it.

For years, it was the only thing Payton would eat.

And not just in the morning.

For lunch too.

She'd been a picky eater, but not because she didn't like food. She loved it. However, her mother had the family cook make some strange things and Payton liked to be a bit on the defiant side at times. One of the ways she got under her mom's skin was to be simple in her food choices.

That extended to clothes as well. No designer bags or shoes for Payton.

"I'm worried about you, pumpkin."

She cringed. She'd always hated it when her father called her that. It was fine when she'd been ten.

But she was thirty-two years old. She owned a ranch. She paid people's salaries and was responsible for herself. She didn't need her father to take care of her, much less call her pet nicknames.

"This is exactly why your mother wants you back here with us."

"No, Dad. Mom wants me to move back because she wants to set me up with someone in your office so I can quit working, like she did, and have babies." Payton held her breath for a moment. She placed her hand over her stomach. If her parents only knew. But she'd never tell them. She'd never hurt her mom that way. The fact that her mother had four miscarriages when all that she'd ever wanted in life was to have a big family had been a painful topic.

Payton understood that. While she and her mom were two completely different people, that didn't take away her mother's hopes and dreams.

But that didn't make those Payton's dreams either.

Just because a woman didn't want to work outside the home, that didn't make her less than a whole person. The choice to raise children was a huge one and it commanded as much respect as the decision to work. The hardest part for Payton when it came to her mom had been the pressure to get married and have kids.

Even in the last month, her mother had sent her

photographs and biographies of her friends' sons who might make good partners. Men who would treat her like an equal and a queen at the same time.

Only, her mom didn't understand what the word equal meant.

Her mother's measurement for a decent, kind man was really someone who would want and encourage their little lady to stay home with the babies. Payton, on the other hand, wanted someone who respected women and their choices. If they wanted to work, it was for their partner to support. Her mom would often say she agreed and understood. That it was for the couple to figure out, but then she'd always say something like, *But if you have the means, you don't have to, so why on earth would you want to. Little boys and girls need their mama.*

It was a doubled-edged sword and Payton didn't think her mom knew how hypocritical her opinions were. That said, kudos to the woman for trying to lend a voice to women's rights.

Because she did.

However, for Roxy, being a full-time mom had been more fulfilling than getting a master's degree or the few years she worked.

Roxy loved being a mother and she desperately wanted to be a grandmother. More than anything else on this earth. It seemed like it was the only thing that mattered. The pressure Payton's mother put on her had become unbearable. The texts about this friend or that who'd just gotten married or had become pregnant and when was that going to be Payton happened weekly. She even started sending her messages about people they barely knew.

Payton also believed her mother loved her. At least on some level, even though her mom could be self-centered and single-minded, but she wasn't a monster.

"You can't blame your mother for wanting that for you. And what father doesn't want to dance with their daughter at their wedding."

"No one is ever saying that I won't get married and have kids; that's not even the point." Though, she'd probably never have a traditional wedding and that would be another disappointment. If and when she were to marry, she'd most likely elope. Or have a small ceremony here at the ranch. A few friends. Her parents. But there would be no big white wedding dress.

Jeans and a flannel would do the trick.

Her eyes went to the newspaper and the headlines. *Alpha Gray Wolf found dead on the Wheeler Creek Ranch. Payton Wheeler is a person of interest in the case.*

She'd been questioned by three different agencies—Wildlife, Yellowstone Rangers, and the sheriff, Joe Sand, who told her point blank that people were gunning for her and to watch her back.

"You're right. It's not. And I can be there by nightfall," her father said.

She reached for her mug and took a sip of coffee. The scalding bitter brew hit the back of her throat like a cattle prod. She coughed. "No. Stay in New York. I don't need you to come save me. I'm a big girl and I can handle things here myself."

"I don't like you out there in that big house all by yourself."

For a brief second, she considered telling him about Justice and the Brotherhood Protectors, but decided that wouldn't be a good idea. If anything, it could put her mother on a plane faster than her dad.

My God. A man staying under the same roof.

That could be cause for celebration. All her mom needed to do was deem him worthy of her baby girl.

The criterion was simple.

He had to be educated and that didn't always mean college, but that was generally the better bet. However, the ability to hold down a decent job and make good money would be enough at this juncture in her life.

The fact that Justice had been in the military for many years would suffice. It was noble. Honorable. And her mom and dad would approve. They would even accept his choice of working with the Brotherhood Protectors. But that might not be good enough for their baby girl.

While it commanded the kind of respect they desired, it didn't pay the salary they coveted.

Nor did the ranch.

The real question would be could Justice be pliable. Meaning would he relocate and learn to work for the other family business.

Oh, good Lord. Why the hell was she even thinking like this? It was fucking ridiculous. She was never leaving the ranch.

"I'm surrounded by macho ranch hands," she said.

"Those men might know a thing or two about cattle and horses. But they're big children, not men, and I don't trust them to take care of my girl." Her father had admitted that he walked away from the Wheeler Creek Ranch for three reasons.

The first, and the most important, was that it wasn't his dream. He didn't want to work on what he considered a farm. It didn't excite him and no one could fault him for that. He got great passion out of creating buildings. High-rises that people could live in. Or work and build their dreams in.

For as long as she could remember, her father had told her that the ranch had never been something he aspired to own. And his father—her grandfather—knew that.

He had no passion for the ranch life. Not even

when he'd been a little boy. He didn't particularly like animals, and it showed. He much preferred creating towns and cities. He thrived when he had a pencil in his hand and sat in front of a drafting board. Or at least that's what he told Payton. By the time she'd been ten years old, he'd stopped using his architectural degree and got into other aspects of Montgomery Development. He stopped creating and building, though he didn't see it that way.

And now that she had some time and space from that business, she realized that while there was a time and place for land developers, they often were short-sided, looking only at what was being created, not destroyed.

The second reason her father left Montana and his heritage had been the fact he'd fallen madly in love with her mother, who vacationed in the area for a couple of summers. Roxy Montgomery Wheeler came from money. And not just any money. Old money. The kind of money that bought wine by the year, not by the price on the bottle, which meant it was more expensive than anyone could generally imagine. And in her circles, that meant her mother had style and class. Her family had created an empire through real estate in New York, Connecticut, New Jersey, Massachusetts, Delaware, and Virginia. There were three generations of wealth.

No one questioned that.

At least not back east.

It didn't work that way in Montana.

Money had a different value in these parts.

Greg Wheeler had been given a choice.

Help his father run a ranch and make a decent—but hard—living.

Or move to New York City where he could take a job and learn his father-in-law's real estate development business and possibly take that over. At Montgomery Development, he could make millions and he could follow a dream.

He could use his talents—or what her grandpa called doodling skills—and design buildings, towns, and parks. Anything Greg Wheeler could think of, he could put on paper and someone could then build it.

It was magic.

It turned into a no-brainer for her father. He was driven by two things.

Love and the fact he thrived in a city environment.

She couldn't fault her dad for that.

But the third reason left a bitter taste in Payton's mouth, and she had to examine it for herself, but it's one of the reasons she opted to work for her father and not move to Montana when she'd graduated college.

And that was power and money.

She'd fallen into that trap as well. It was hard

not to considering how she was raised. The best of everything had been given to her just because her mother had been a Montgomery. Her mother had been the daughter of William S. Montgomery. The grandson of the founder of Montgomery Development. The company that brought you malls, hospitals, and condominiums. Whatever your community needed, Montgomery could build it. They'd been a staple in the northeast for over a hundred years.

Much like the Wheelers had been a part of Montana and Wyoming.

When she stepped out on the town, people noticed. It had been both a blessing and a curse. As a small child, she didn't understand the significance, but when she'd been in college, she wished people had no clue as to who she was. She felt as though she lived in a fishbowl. However, that all changed when she went to work at Montgomery Development. So many doors were open for her professionally and she dived right into her work.

During the day, she was Greg Wheeler's daughter. She was the pride and joy of the company.

At night, she reminisced of the past. Of the big Montana sky.

It had seemed like a lifetime ago.

And then there was Davey. The pain over giving him up had still been so fresh. Worse, the father—and older man—had married and had a child. He had no use for Payton. Part of her needed to heal from the past and she did so by diving into a future she had thought she wanted nothing to do with and yet she believed it had given her purpose.

Only, all it did was allow her to hide from everything that really mattered to her.

"Please let us come. Or better yet, come home. This is where you belong," her father said.

For years, Payton had been torn as to what path to take. Even after she'd given up her child, she wasn't sure if she'd stay in New York or go to Montana. It wasn't until her junior year that she finally made that decision. Not because she loved money more than anything else, but because it was what she understood best and of course, she wanted to avoid certain memories.

She'd lived in her mother's world all her life, where she'd only visited the Wheeler Creek Ranch. She'd been an interloper.

And still was—at least according to everyone in Montana.

She hadn't thought that way about her mother's heritage and no one in Montgomery Development had treated her that way. Or so she thought.

That was until she'd spent some time working there and she'd learned she didn't belong in that environment either.

The ranch was her home. It's where she fit in, where she felt comfortable, and she was determined to have everyone else know it too. Her grandfather had told her that it had taken him years before he'd earned the respect of his father's employees.

That's how it worked.

Just because you inherited a piece of property or a business or whatever, that didn't mean you inherited the honor and respect that came with it. Nope. A person needed to step up and prove their worth. It wasn't about filling their predecessor's shoes, but making them their own.

Her problem had not only been that she hadn't been raised under the big sky, but that the only person she had in her corner who counted was dead.

With her grandfather gone, the tension with Hosa Ezhno and his wife Kimi had become a little more heated.

They wanted to expand their lodging, but that meant using the access road, and her grandfather didn't want cars traveling through that part of his land in part because he herded cattle from one pasture to another and also because he believed it would change the landscape.

Payton didn't necessarily agree. There was a part of her that considered opening up a campground, but that was more of a three-year plan. Or at least when things settled down and she had a better handle on things.

"No, Daddy. Grandpa trusted me with this ranch and I love it here. This is what I want and I'm not going to let someone scare me off. You raised me to stand up for myself. That's what I'm doing."

"I'm proud of you. I really am. It takes courage to pack up and move across the country." Her father's voice was laced with thick emotion. It trembled with every syllable. "But your mom. She's beside herself. She's worried sick about you."

Payton had often felt suffocated by her mother's love. It was the kind of love that came with a price tag. It wasn't conditional, so to speak, because no matter what, Payton felt loved. She knew her mom cared deeply. Maybe too deep. The amount of affection her mother was willing to give was in direct correlation with Payton's decisions. If her mom approved, then all was good in the world. If she didn't, well, her mom knew how to hold a grudge.

She sighed.

She needed to accept the fact that her mother did hold her love hostage. That didn't make her mom a bad person. Her mom wanted certain things from life and she demanded her family respect her wishes.

"And to be honest, I have to admit, with all that is happening, so am I. It's a different world out there. They have a different code that they live by.

Even I'm considered an outsider now and I was born and raised there."

"There are a lot of people who come here and make Montana their home. I'll be accepted. I have to stay the course." She leaned back in her chair. The sound of the front door closing caught her attention.

It had been so quiet, she almost forgot she had company.

She glanced at the clock on the wall.

Eight in the morning.

She'd stepped outside and had chatted with Davey for about a half hour. That had been around seven thirty.

She wondered what time Justice woke and where he'd been. Who had he talked to? What had he found out?

Did he have breakfast? Coffee? Had he had a shower yet?

Christ.

That last thought she needed like she needed another restless night.

"Besides, aren't you the one who told me that you weren't greeted with open arms the moment you landed in Manhattan? That you were tested at every turn and people didn't trust you and did things to undermine you?"

"You're right. All that is true. But most people in this city aren't carrying guns and get their point across with violence," her dad said. "I know you loved your grandpa. And I'm sorry that he and I didn't have a great relationship for your sake. But this isn't how you prove your love for him. You can sell the ranch. I'm sure there are a number of buyers ready—"

"I'm not selling." She pulled off another small piece of her bagel and shoved it in her mouth. She had to keep her parents from getting on a plane. For as long as she could remember, her parents had always tried to make her decisions. One summer they even went as far as to try to cancel her trip out west.

Her grandfather put a stop to that, thankfully.

She understood they wanted the best for their daughter, but what they failed to take into consideration was that their vision for her future didn't match up to Payton's desires. She did what her parents had planned for her life, not what she had dreamed about doing since she'd been a ten-year-old little girl.

Now that she had the chance to follow her dreams, she wasn't going to let her parents bully her out of this opportunity because they couldn't—wouldn't—relinquish control. She felt like her father generally played Switzerland, and sometimes it appeared like he privately took her side and did what he could to persuade her mom.

But not this time.

Looking back on her life, when it came to where she went to college or what she did with her life careerwise, her parents called the shots.

"That kind of life is hard," her father said. "Your grandfather was only seventy-three when he died. That ranch put him into the grave early. Not to mention that it's a difficult way to earn a living."

"You know as well as I do that the Wheeler Creek Ranch is financially healthy, so let's not have that conversation again." She was tired of listening to how much more she'd earn if she stayed in Manhattan. It didn't matter to her that she gave up millions to run a ranch that would only net her half her salary at the other family business. "I'm not going to keep having the same argument with you, Dad." She glanced up and smiled at Justice, who stood in the doorway with a tall mug of something steaming from the top.

He leaned against the doorjamb and smiled back.

Her heart dropped to her gut.

Damn.

She'd noticed him last night, but she hadn't gotten the full picture with his broad shoulders and thick biceps with ink all up and down his arms.

He hadn't shaved and she liked the scruffy look on him.

Truthfully, she more than liked a lot about Justice. He was everything that she had been told not to like in a man and that made him even more appealing.

But mostly, he'd been nothing short of a gentleman. He'd been kind, considerate, and damn freaking sweet.

"If you're not going to sell, then what are you doing to protect yourself? Because I can't leave my little girl out there all alone."

Shit. She told herself she wasn't going to say a single word about the Brotherhood Protectors. But she didn't want her father showing up unannounced either, and the longer she talked to her dad, the more she realized she didn't have a choice. "I'm not alone, Daddy. You don't need to worry. I hired a professional."

"A professional what? And why didn't you tell me that at the start of this conversation? You could have saved me a ton of aggravation."

"A bodyguard and I didn't tell you because I didn't want to have this discussion, but if it will keep you from coming, then so be it."

Justice arched a brow as he blew into his mug.

She didn't understand why he gave her such an amused look. That's exactly what he'd been hired to do.

"Seriously?" her father asked. "Who? What do you know about this person? Are you sure they are legit?"

"Yes, Dad. He's from an organization called the

Brotherhood Protectors. They are all ex-military. If —and this is a big if—someone is trying to hurt me, they will have to go through him, and trust me, he's like a gladiator or something."

Justice covered his mouth and stifled a laugh.

She glared.

"I guess that makes me feel better and I'll pass that on to your mother. But you better call me if something happens. I will be on the first plane out there. Or better yet, we can put that place on the market."

"Goodbye, Dad. I love you."

"Seriously, young lady—"

"Dad. I've got to go. I'll call if there's a problem."

"You better," her father said. "I love you, too."

She set the phone on the table, keeping her gaze on her bagel. She wasn't sure if it was the conversation with her father that had made her feel like she wanted to jump out of her skin.

Or the man standing and staring at her.

"I'm not sure anyone has ever described me as a gladiator before," Justice said as he made himself comfortable in the chair next to hers.

She swallowed, hoping that would give her the courage to lift her gaze. "I'm trying to keep my parents from hopping the next flight out from New York."

"I can speak to them if you want because I don't

want them here either. That's just more people I have to keep track of, making my job harder."

"If something else happens, my dad might lose his shit, and then I might need you to do that."

"Do you tell your father everything?" Justice took a big swig of his coffee before setting his mug on the table. He folded his massive arms and rested them on the wood surface, staring at her intently with his ice-blue eyes.

"Yes and no."

"I don't believe you can split that question down the middle."

"I tell him most things," she admitted. "I've always been close to my parents, for the most part."

"I'm going to ask you not to tell him, or anyone, what's going on or what I'm doing or not doing."

She jerked her head. "Why not?" On the one hand, what she chose to tell her parents, or not tell them, was no one's business. And there were a lot of things over the years that she had kept from them.

Namely, Davey.

But she didn't like being told what she could or couldn't tell them when it came to her safety.

"We can't afford leaks. Not with the headlines."

"What the hell is that supposed to mean? We're talking about my parents. Who are in Manhattan, by the way." She appreciated how Justice took his job seriously; however, he seemed to be a bit over the top.

He reached across the table and rested his hand over hers.

Intense heat scorched across her skin, covering every inch from her fingertips to her toes. It seeped into her veins, making its way to her heart where it exploded like fireworks on the Fourth of July.

She tried to swallow, but her throat muscles wouldn't work properly. She blinked, doing her best to keep her focus, but it was difficult when all she wanted to do was kiss his lips.

"I'm not suggesting anything bad about your mom and dad. I'm only saying that we can't afford to have whoever has been harassing you and possibly whoever may have shot the gray wolf get the upper hand."

When he put it that way, she had to agree.

"Okay. I won't say anything to them but understand it will be hard. My folks call daily. I have to tell them something."

"Then tell them things are quiet. Tell them my presence must have scared whoever has been doing the bad things away."

"I think I can do that."

"Good," Justice said. "However, I do have some bad news to tell you."

She sucked in a deep breath. "What's that?"

"I did a sweep of the house for bugs, and I found two."

She gasped. The idea someone could be listening to her phone calls, her conversations with Trapper, Daisy, or anyone else for that matter, made her shiver. "How is that possible?"

"I spoke with Colin, your foreman. He said that in the last few months your grandfather was alive, he was paranoid. It's possible he put them in and no has been listening, but it's also possible that in the days between when your grandpa died and you moved here, any number of people could have planted them."

"I suppose all of that is a fair statement, especially that my grandpa had grown incredibly suspicious of people. He told me that sometimes his way of life clashed with modern life, though I wasn't quite sure what that meant other than he didn't trust some people."

"Do you know who, specifically?"

"Truthfully?" Payton rolled her neck. She hated vocalizing this reality because all it did was bring up old pains. "My parents."

"Why?"

"I wish I knew. The only thing I can tell you is that my grandfather didn't particularly care for my mom or her family, and my dad and his father were like oil and water."

"Colin, your foreman, told me that no one had

any idea that Eddy was going to leave the ranch to you, including your parents. Did you know?"

She shook her head. "My grandfather never mentioned it. I assumed my grandpa would leave it to his business manager, Topper, and his wife."

"Why not your father?"

"My dad didn't want it and he made that clear. He doesn't appreciate what the land stands for. What all this means. He left the first chance he got and he never looked back. My grandfather didn't leave it to him because he knew he'd sell it. I think my mom and dad were confused by why he didn't leave it to Topper, though."

"And is Topper confused? Because I got the vibe from Colin that everyone thought that Topper would be taking over."

"I think it's safe to say the world was shocked that I was named as sole owner of the ranch." She held up her hand. "I expected something. A percentage. Money. I knew I'd be named in some capacity. But then again, the last year of my grandfather's life, he used to call me and say things like, some day when the ranch was mine. When I would ask him specifically about that, he'd laugh and remind me that we had the same last name."

"So, what you're telling me is that he told you that he planned on leaving you the ranch; you just never caught on."

"I guess you could look at it that way." She'd

replayed so many conversations she'd had with her grandfather over the last few months before he'd passed. Mostly they discussed her lack of a love life and the fact most men she not only found boring as sin, but they weren't even close to being the kind of person she would consider spending her life with. Granted, she was picky as hell and wanted a partner.

An equal.

In every sense of the word. She didn't want to be with someone who treated her like the little woman.

It wasn't necessarily about equal division of assets. Or who did what around the house. It was about mutual respect.

A comradery.

She wanted someone who valued what she brought to the table and appreciated her hopes and dreams and supported her as much as she supported him.

So far, she hadn't found it.

However, she honestly hadn't looked that hard. The relationships she'd had in the city fell short of passionate. They met her physical needs, but they did nothing to fulfill anything else and oftentimes made her feel as though she were a robot of sorts.

"When I was named, Topper called me and told me he'd support me."

"Did you—do you—believe him?" Justice asked.

"I do," she said with conviction. "Even though he often tells me I'm wrong, or we butt heads about something, he never does that in front of people. He's respectful. He loved my grandfather like family. He wants what is best for this ranch and he's loyal to a fault."

Justice gave her hand a good squeeze. "I don't know who put in the bugs. Or how long they have been there. I will be interviewing everyone who works here, but no one is to know we found them. And I still need to search your bedroom."

"Where were the bugs found?"

"The family room and your office."

"So someone could have been listening to us last night?" She rubbed her hands over her thighs.

"That's possible, which means the bad guys already know I'm here."

"I take it that's not good," she said.

"It's not ideal. I would have liked to have blended in."

She chuckled. "I'm sorry. You don't blend in. You stand out."

"What? You don't think I look like a cowboy?" He glanced up and down at himself. It was the first time she'd seen him smile and relax.

She liked the softer side of Justice.

Maybe a little too much.

"You might be able to pass as one, but everyone here knows each other. It's a small town, and let's just say you are quite memorable. Besides, the Brotherhood Protector organization is all the buzz in West Yellowstone these days."

"I want to believe you're giving me a compliment, but I'm not exactly sure."

Heat rose to her cheeks. They felt as though they were on fire. "Yeah." She fanned herself. "You'd have to be dead not to notice you, so in one way, it's a compliment."

"Thank you," he said. "So, what's the dig?"

"Well, can you do all the cowboy things?"

"I can ride a horse," he said with a fair amount of confidence and a wide smile. "I've tried roping and I suck at it. I won't go near a bull unless my life depended on it. I don't know much about moving cattle, but I did help push them from one field to another before. However, I do know a lot about tracking animals. I'm an expert in search and rescue. So, I think I could manage to find a way to fit in if I had to."

"But now that the bugs have been found and whoever knows that you're here, you don't have to." She shivered. This threat was real. Maybe they didn't mean her physical harm, but they sure as hell meant something. She crossed her arms over her chest. "Can they hear us now?" she whispered.

"No." He scooted his chair closer and rested his hand on her shoulder.

His touch was gentle. Tender. And that

surprised her. Based on what he'd told her last night, and his appearance, he seemed like a hardened man, not someone who could understand, much less feel, another person's emotions.

But he did.

"However, from here on in, the circle of trust is small. Very small."

"What do you mean by that?"

"I trust my team. And no one else. Not even Colin, who called the Brotherhood Protectors and knows one of my buddies."

"I don't think he could have anything to do with this, especially killing a gray wolf," she said.

"Probably not, but that's not the point. Colin has access to this house. So does Daisy and Topper as well as the chef. They all have keys and can come and go as they please. That means they could have planted the bugs."

"The maid, Sandy, also has a key."

"So, you get where I'm coming from."

Unfortunately, she did. "What you're telling me is for now, I can't talk to them about this. Or anyone for that matter."

"You can talk to me. The rest, we have to tell them some things for their safety and ours. However, we don't tell anyone about the bugs. Or what we did with them. If I want to feed information to someone about what we find during our investigation, I'll let you know what can be shared.

When I've fully vetted someone, you'll know they've been pulled into our inner circle. This includes your folks." He tapped the newspaper. "These headlines hurt your reputation, and since there was already some animosity, it will make it worse. And social media is buzzing with what happened. Until I figure out a few things, we keep what we know to ourselves."

"But we barely know anything," she said with a tremble in her throat. When she'd first landed in Montana after her grandfather died, she'd felt alone. Lost. A bit in the dark. Topper hadn't helped much since he'd been cold and distant. It didn't matter that he'd done his job. He still kept a safe distance.

He'd become more supportive and that happened before the shit started.

She had Colin and Daisy, but they had each other, and because of their relationship, they tended to keep to themselves anyway.

Outside of that, Payton felt like an interloper.

She could live with that and she made the most of it.

However, nothing could prepare her for the utter emptiness she had growing in the pit of her stomach right now.

"How can we figure things out if it's you and me against the world?"

His hand ran up and down her biceps in a

soothing motion. It calmed her wild pulse and eased her painful breath. "My buddy, Wade, isn't working an assignment right now. He and I grew up together. He's saved my life literally a good dozen times. He's going to be helping me by being a second set of eyes on everything that comes our way and by doing research and helping me handle interviews. He'll observe where I can't since it's not possible for me to be in two places at one time. I don't trust anyone like I trust him."

"Does he work for the Brotherhood Protectors too?"

"He does," Justice said. "Wade was there for me when no one else was and he'll be there for you now. However, I need to search your room before this day gets away from us. And then, I want the full tour. I want to meet everyone. I also want you to introduce me to everyone as your bodyguard. I want to see the staff's reaction."

"Let's get this party started." She pressed her hands against the table and stood. "How good of a rider are you?"

"Average," he said.

"For a city slicker or for a cowboy?"

"One second you're stoking my ego, the next second I feel totally inadequate," he said with a chuckle. "I don't look silly on a horse. Let's leave it at that."

"I'll have the stall boy saddle up Dumplin' for you."

Justice stood and pushed his chair to the table. He lowered his chin. "What's your horse's name?"

"Bourbon," she said, smiling wide.

"I think I can handle a horse with a name like Bourbon."

"No. Dumplin' is more your style. Trust me."

"As long as you never tell anyone." He ran a hand over the top of his head. "I'll never hear the end of it."

"It's just a name."

"So is Justice, but there is something poetic about it."

CHAPTER 5

Justice dismounted Dumplin', grateful he hadn't made a complete fool of himself and even more thankful that Payton had given him such a friendly horse. Almost too friendly. She liked to say hello to everyone and everything.

But she wasn't temperamental and that was a good thing.

"I'll take it from here, sir," the stall boy said.

"Your name is Davey, right?" Justice had learned from a young age to remember details. Names, phones numbers, important dates, and appointments all had to be memorized. His father hadn't provided him with a laptop, tablet, or smart phone. If he wanted those things, he had to save to buy them himself. However, when he did, his dad would often confiscate them, so he'd have to hide them. That wasn't an easy task outside of the school year where he could leave things in his locker.

Or sometimes he'd *forget* things at Wade's house who would charge them for him, but still, Justice had to have a mind for detail.

"Yes, sir. And you're the bodyguard."

"You can call me Justice."

Davey nodded.

"How old are you, kid?"

"Fourteen." Davey took the horse by the reins.

"And you work here?" Justice followed the boy around the pen as he cooled down Dumplin'.

"I do, sir," Davey said. "My parents purchase show horses for Grandpa Wheeler. They also ride in rodeos under the Wheeler Ranch name. My dad's also a horse breeder."

Justice filed everything the boy said but got stuck on one key phrase. "You called him Grandpa?"

Davey shrugged. "Sometimes when my parents travel together, I stay here at the ranch. I don't have any grandparents, so I guess I kind of started calling him that on my own when I was little. He said it was okay with him if it was okay with my folks. They were okay with it, so it stuck."

"That makes sense," Justice said. "How did Payton feel about you calling her grandfather —grandpa."

"She's always been kind to me. Still is. I like her

and she's never said anything to me about it one way or the other."

"What about her parents? Did they have a problem with it?"

"I don't really know them at all. Whenever they came to visit, they kind of kept to themselves. Sometimes they stayed in town in one of the more expensive hotels while Payton stayed her with her grandfather alone."

Justice thought that was interesting. He didn't have a good handle on family dynamics. His were shitty, but he did have a basic understanding of what positive family relationships looked like thanks to Wade and his family.

But the truth was, he didn't have any comprehension of anything but extremes. He grew up with fist sandwiches, while Wade grew up in a loving environment.

Justice hadn't been exposed to much of the in between.

But that didn't mean it didn't exist and Wade constantly told him—as did his other teammates— about how dysfunction didn't mean bad and that just because sometimes family didn't speak to each other didn't mean they didn't care was a common theme in most families.

Perhaps this was an example of that.

"Did they get along with Grandpa Wheeler?" Justice asked.

Davey laughed as he paused in front of the opening of the barn. "That's not an easy question to answer honestly."

"Why?"

"The few times they hung out at the ranch, it appeared they got along more for Payton's sake," Davey said. "But she and her grandpa had a unique relationship. I envied it, so when I found out he left this place to her and not Topper, I did a little happy dance."

"You don't like Topper?"

Davey raised his hand. "Oh. No. He's cool. I like him just fine. I just don't see him running this place the same way as Grandpa Wheeler and Payton. You have to give her credit for trying to keep things to tradition, and yet, she's also doing her darndest to make this ranch her own. I like working for her."

Justice bit down on the inside of his cheek to keep from smiling. The boy admired Payton. Respected her.

Well, Justice couldn't blame the kid.

"Do you think there is anyone on the ranch who would want to hurt Payton? Or see her leave?"

"Most people have had their reservations about Payton and if she would stick it out. This isn't for everyone, but no one that I know of dislikes her or wants to see her fail. At least not on the ranch," Davey said.

"What about the employees that quit? I heard they had a lot to say about Payton."

"You're talking about Tim, Reemy, and James and they just didn't like taking orders from a woman. Lots of people out here are like that. My dad says people here still think this is a man's world, but that is a narrow-minded way of thinking."

"Your dad's a smart man," Justice said. "Do you know where they are working now?" He hadn't planned on pumping a teenager for information, but this kid not only had an old soul, but he had a hardened heart that came with living in the real world when he should have been playing on the jungle gym in the backyard. He was wise beyond his years.

"They were offered positions with Hosa Ezhno, but they didn't take the jobs."

From what Justice understood, Hosa had issues with both Payton and her grandfather over the access road.

"Do you know why?"

"Because the pay was a lot less than what they were making here. James is officially retiring and moving to Arizona to be closer to his grandkids. I have no idea what Timothy and Reemy are doing. I can't say I liked them very much, but I don't believe they would do anything to hurt Payton."

Davey had implied that twice now. Either he really believed that or he wanted Justice to.

Either way, the three ex-employees were still suspects.

But Justice wasn't sure where to file this young man. He flew so low under the radar that he should be suspicious of him.

Fuck. Davey was a kid. But he'd have to keep him on the list for the simple reason he called Eddy Grandpa Wheeler and had left the boy ten thousand dollars.

That alone was cause for concern. He and his family could be under the assumption the ranch should have been willed to them, not Payton. He didn't get that impression and it would take a lot of composure for a kid to lie this well, but that didn't mean his parents weren't the culprits.

"Thanks for the information and the help with the horse," Justice said.

"You're welcome." The boy gave him a quick nod. "Please keep Payton safe. I'd hate for anything bad to happen to her."

That got Justice wondering what would happen to the ranch if something did.

He stuffed his hands in his pockets and strolled toward the house. The sun had started its decent behind the mountains. Justice had always loved being in wide-open spaces. He felt safe in the middle of nowhere under a blanket of stars. He never liked being in a crowd of people or on a busy street.

Small-town living had been the only way he could breathe.

His cell vibrated in his back pocket. He pulled it out.

Wade.

"Hey, man. Does my work husband miss me already?"

"Are you kidding me," Wade said. "I don't have to listen to you snore or have anyone steal my bacon. I'm in heaven."

"I would never steal a man's meat."

"Do you hear yourself?"

Justice laughed. "What's up?"

"Did you read the report from the wildlife doctor?"

"I've only had a chance to skim it. I've been out interviewing everyone on the ranch today. Most people have an enormous amount of respect for Payton, though not all believe she could pull off running the place. Some still worry she won't go the distance, but they need their jobs so they either keep their heads down and do their jobs or go out of their way to help her."

"Well, the key aspect of that report was the fact that the doctor stated it's possible the wolf did not die in that spot."

"Yeah. I saw that. But it's only because the bullet

wound isn't believed to have been fatal. But the Yellowstone ranger thought there should have been a blood trail if the wolf stumbled to its death," Justice said. "Not to mention the wildlife agent's report is a little different. He really doesn't like Payton and he's on my *look at more closely* list."

"I've got something else for you to consider," Wade said. "Topper took out a million-dollar business loan two months ago."

"Does he have a side hustle?"

"His wife does. She has a small retail gift shop in town and she makes candles. But not to the tune of a million dollars."

"Unless maybe she's in trouble," Justice said. "All the more reason Topper might be pissed that he wasn't willed the ranch. Or at least a percentage of the profits. Or something. All he got was artwork. He's still my number one suspect."

"It gets better," Wade said. "I've learned that Topper had a thing for Greg's wife back in the day."

"Roxy didn't grow up in Montana. Her family only vacationed here." Justice rubbed his temple as he climbed the front steps. His breath grew darker in the cold winter air. He loved this climate. It's one of the reasons when the Brotherhood Protectors called his team, he was the first one nodding yes. His entire life had been shaped by the cold and while so many people enjoyed the sun and the beaches, he'd take a snowy hilltop any day of the week. He swore his blood was made with icicles.

"They had a timeshare there for years and Topper even took her out on a couple of dates."

"Are you serious?"

"I've heard from people in the know that he had eyes for her, but that she didn't give him more than a quick glance."

"Everyone that I've spoken to has mentioned that Roxy Montgomery had her sights set on Greg Wheeler from the get-go."

"Well, there's something more important for us to think about," Wade said. "I spoke with a business associate of Roxy's father who retired years ago. He told me that her dad had been trying to buy land in Montana. He wanted his own dude ranch. Something to cater to the rich and famous. An all-inclusive spa, hotel, experience like nothing else. He'd been talking with a couple of land owners, but the Wheeler Creek Ranch was prime location for him. It's possible that Roxy's father put her up to the union."

"Whatever came of the idea to turn this place into a resort?"

"According to my source, once Greg and Roxy became a hot and heavy item, Greg talked his future father-in-law out of the idea. Besides, Eddy Wheeler wasn't going to sell, and Greg didn't think it was the right location. My sources said he thought something closer to West Yellowstone might have been better. However, this is where it gets weird," Wade said. "Topper wanted the sale or at the very least, a partnership. He thought turning the Wheeler Creek Ranch into a dude ranch would be good, but not a resort. Topper has indicated that he doesn't agree with hotels, especially posh ones. He likes campgrounds, yurts, rustic lodging. Anything that gives people the Wild West experience."

"I'm getting ready to meet with Topper right now. I'll ask him about that." Justice curled his fingers around the doorknob. "But it was thirty years ago. Is there anything in your research that tells you that someone wasn't able to move beyond the past?"

"No. The only red flag I have is that loan by Topper. I'm going to head into Cooke City tomorrow and check out his wife's shop. I'll be in touch."

"Thanks. I appreciate it."

"Stay out of trouble," Wade said.

"Never," Justice said, then tapped the red button, ending the call.

While everyone described Eddy Wheeler as a generous man—and in many ways he was—his will didn't indicate that at all, with a few exceptions, two that stood out.

He left the boy a small amount of money.

And he left a woman in town by the name of Monica Lewis his antique car collection and ten thousand dollars. Turns out, he'd been having an affair with Monica for years, so that made sense and even Payton didn't question the gift.

However, Justice did.

More so, he wondered how Monica felt about Payton being left everything else and he planned on having a chat with Monica as well. This was the part of his new job that didn't come naturally. He never considered himself a people person. He was fine with his brothers-in-arms, but outside of that, he had to step way out of his comfort zone. Holding interviews, interrogating, those things other members of his team had done. Gabe had wicked communication skills. Edge was a man of few words, but he could get people talking. Ridge was just intimidating as hell sometimes and it worked for him. Wade, however, had a unique way of making people feel comfortable. And it was genuine.

Justice would rather Wade do this part, but Justice would have to figure it out because while they were still a team in every sense of the word, their assignments wouldn't always be as one.

Something Justice had to personally come to terms with.

He crossed the threshold of Payton's home. He still wanted to do a second check for listening devices, even though he'd only found the two. Better to be safe than sorry.

Making his way to the den behind the staircase, he did his best to categorize all the information floating around in his brain, focusing on what related to Topper.

A fifty-seven-year-old male with two kids of his own and a couple of grandkids. He wasn't a wealthy man and so far, Justice hadn't found anything disturbing about the man. Everyone on the ranch knew what Justice was doing and why. He'd lost the element of surprise. He couldn't pretend to be anything else and while that gave him the opportunity to ask anything, it also gave everyone the chance to perfect their stories.

His bullshit meter and lie detector was going to have to be on high alert.

He opened the laptop on the desk and pulled up the copy of the last will and testament that Payton had forwarded. He found the paragraph that related specifically to a few items and livestock that were given out to the major players.

Topper had been willed expensive artwork valued at about fifty grand.

Daisy had been left her horse and a couple of pieces of jewelry that had been Payton's grand-mother's. Payton had told him she was perfectly fine with it. She wasn't a flashy person and Daisy had always admired the pieces.

Colin had been given Eddy's wedding ring and a horse.

Seemed like Payton's grandfather liked giving away horses. Then again, the ranch bought them every season.

The chef had been given a set of knives and the maid one of the extra vacuum cleaners along with a piece of art.

Monica, of course, had been left money and the cars.

But nowhere in the will was there mention of Greg or Roxy Wheeler.

Not even their names.

That was odd.

Justice leaned back in the chair and clasped his hands behind his head. There was no love lost between him and his old man. Justice honestly didn't care if he ever saw his dad again. Although, that made him sad. Not so much because he had deep-rooted feelings for his father. He thought maybe he loved his dad, out of obligation. But not the kind of love a son normally felt.

Same went for his mom.

Deep down, Justice wished his parents had loved him, but they didn't and there was no point in trying to pretend otherwise. He didn't have blinders on and he wasn't bitter.

He was realistic about his childhood and how that formed him as a man. It made him loyal to those who did deserve his friendship and his love. He gave that family commitment to Wade first, and then once they both joined the Army, it slowly seeped over to their first special forces team. He'd created in the military what he should have gotten from his mom and dad. He had no malice in his heart.

Not anymore.

However, he did have a touch of sadness.

Not just for himself, but for every young boy who didn't have the kind of nurturing homelife that his true brother, Wade, had.

Kids like Davey.

Because when you don't have someone to teach you how to love with an open mind, soul, and heart, you can become hard and rotten.

Justice had been one of the lucky ones—thanks to Wade and his family.

He closed the laptop and made his way to the kitchen where he snagged himself a soda. No sooner did he close the fridge than the bell rang, followed by the door opening.

"Hello?" Topper called out.

"In the kitchen," Justice said as he made himself comfortable at the small table with his drink and a bag of pretzels. He had a few questions that he'd settled on in his mind, but as Wade always told him, he needed to trust his instincts. To go with his gut. "Come on back and thanks for using the bell."

"So, you're living in the house," Topper said with a fair amount of disdain in his tone. "I thought you were staying in the bunkhouse. Or barn."

That was a weird statement because he'd been under the impression that Topper wanted him close by. As in it had been him—among others—to suggest he stay in the house.

"I thought you wanted me to protect Payton."

"I do." Topper appeared in the kitchen. He leaned against the doorjamb and sighed. "However, I don't appreciate having your organization look into my finances." He lowered his chin. "This is a small town, and I don't believe you understand how things work."

"Oh. I get it." He lifted his cell and texted Wade that there was a leak somewhere. Probably the bank officers and it might be an innocent passing of intel, but still. It was something Wade could look into on his visit to Cooke City. "I'm looking into everyone who works on this ranch. Anyone who might benefit from Payton being gone. Not just you, so don't take it personally." Justice leaned back and waved his hand. "Please. Have a seat."

Topper chuckled. "You've made yourself at home."

"I wouldn't say that," Justice said. "I have a job to do."

Topper ran a hand over his chin. "I thought

having you here would make people feel safe. Instead, it's having the opposite effect."

"How so?"

"Everyone was already on edge, between their concern for Payton's safety with the threats and now the shooting of the gray wolf. But you come in and start treating everyone like a suspect. You're not a cop, but you're still making everyone nervous."

"Good. Maybe whoever is doing this will fuck up."

Topper shook his head. "Perhaps Colin made a mistake."

"Look." Justice folded his hands and rested them on the table. "I'm not here to make friends. I'm here to solve a problem. I don't care if you like the way I'm doing it or not. I don't work for you. I work for Payton. I answer only to her."

"Well, I'll be sure to have a conversation with her as soon as she returns my call because all you are doing is making enemies. This is not how we do things here. Maybe it's how it's done in the military, but—"

"We can argue about this another time," Justice said. "For now, I want to know what the loan was for."

"That's none of your business." Topper folded his arms across his chest. "But since you and your organization are going to keep digging into my personal business, I'll answer."

"Thank you." Justice wasn't about to tell him that he'd still poke around into the man's life. He assumed Topper was smart enough to figure that one out all by himself.

"My wife had a business partner. A woman she'd known since college. Her name is Leanne Mintz. Unfortunately, Leanne made some questionable decisions, and it left my wife with product we couldn't sell. I had to help bail them out and I didn't want to do it with personal funds. That loan was for my wife to buy out Leanne, which she has. Now she's doing her best to pay it off and make her shop become profitable once again."

That sounded reasonable, but Justice was going to need some confirmation on that.

"I hope it works out for her," Justice said.

"It will, but I don't need you stirring up trouble."

Justice held out his hands. "That's the opposite of what I'm doing and since I know you're a busy man, I'd like to move on to the next topic. What can you tell me about Monica Lewis?"

"Not much to tell there," Topper said. "She and Eddy had a love affair for about ten years. The first couple of years it wasn't anything but physical and they kept it secret. But later, it was out in the open."

"Did she ever live at the ranch?"

Topper shook his head. "She didn't like ranch

life." He chuckled. "They were like the odd couple, but they cared for each other, so it worked in an odd way."

"What about Payton? Did Monica like her? How well did they know each other?" Justice had yet to discuss this with Payton, but he would. Right now, he wanted to know what people on the outside, looking in thought.

"Monica adored Payton. Has always thought of her as family but respected that this was a family ranch and Monica was the interloper. Not Payton," Topper said. "Both Monica and Eddy lost the loves of their lives. Neither one wanted to get married again or live with anyone. They each had their own separate lives. It worked for them."

"You know a lot about their relationship."

"I do," Topper said. "I'm the ranch manager. I know a lot of things." He arched a brow. "What else do you want to know?"

"I'd like to talk about the history between you and Greg Wheeler."

Topper laughed. "You want to know if I'm bitter over Roxy, is that it?"

"I do."

"I'm not," Topper said. "I had a crush on Roxy, like half the county did back in the day." He let his hands drop to his lap. His shoulders lowered as if he were more relaxed. "She had to be the prettiest, most sophisticated young woman these parts had ever seen. She had all us young cowboys mesmerized. And she walked about town like she was flower waiting for a bee to buzz around."

"You were a cowboy back then?"

"I started out in the bunkhouse and then became the foreman."

"Doesn't the foreman live in the bunkhouse?"

"He does and I lived there until I met and married my wife when I was twenty-four, then I moved into the house on the hill where shortly after I was promoted to ranch manager and eventually bought a house closer to town where my wife's family lives."

"Daisy and Colin live in the house on the hill, right?"

"Daisy moved out of the bunkhouse about a month ago. Colin has lived there for a while now. Normally, it's reserved for the manager, but it was empty and there was no reason for him not to live there."

"Is Colin next in line for your job?" Justice asked, wishing he had a notebook and pen. He had an excellent memory, but still, taking notes might be helpful.

"You'd have to ask that question of Payton."

"Okay. What about retirement? You're not that old, but when do you plan on leaving this line of work?"

"My wife would love it if I retired at sixty, but

realistically, we're looking at sixty-five. If Payton will keep me on that long."

"Is there a reason she wouldn't?"

"Not that I know of," Topper said. "We get along well enough, though we don't always see eye to eye, and I won't ever be the kind of manager who bites his tongue. That wouldn't do anyone any good, especially Payton."

"Let's backtrack a bit. How long did you live on the ranch?"

"Until my wife got pregnant with our first kid. She prefers living in town and closer to her family. I tried to talk her into staying. Eddy said I could put an addition on the North Pole—that's the name we call what you're referring to as the house on the hill—but Julie just needed friends and family and this ranch didn't provide that for her."

"So you moved and committed."

Topper nodded.

Now that some of the animosity between Topper and Justice seemed to have calmed, it was time to ask the real tough questions and see what happened. "Why did Greg leave Montana and why didn't Eddy leave his son the ranch?"

"Those are two very different answers," Topper said. "Greg left because he was a money-hungry asshole and saw dollar signs bigger than the Montana sky when he met Roxy."

"You don't think he loves her?"

"I didn't say that." Topper cocked his head. "But Greg never fit in on this ranch. He was like a fish out of water even when he was a young boy. Everyone in the bunkhouse used to pick on him, especially when Eddy forced Greg to move in there."

Justice arched a brow. That sounded cruel. Almost abusive. "Why would the son of the ranch owner live in the bunkhouse with the rest of the employees?"

"Because Eddy believed that no one was above hard work. As a matter of fact, Eddy lived there when he was sixteen for about a year. He said it was the best way to learn how the ranch and the ranch hands functioned."

"How did Greg handle that?"

"The same way he handled everything. With a chip on his shoulder. Greg thought he was better than all of us."

"Is he like that now?"

Topper shrugged. "I don't know. He and I aren't friends anymore and other than his father's funeral, he hasn't spent that much time here."

"But Payton used to come visit each summer."

Topper smiled like a proud uncle. "She did." He nodded. "Greg would put her on a plane—all by herself—and we'd go pick her up at the airport and fly her here by chopper. Or if he and his wife did come with her, they would often go stay at a five-star resort. Payton was such a curious kid. And very outgoing. Full of questions. I don't think she missed her parents all that much either way."

But Justice got the impression they were close. At least that is how Payton presented her relationship with her folks.

This was all interesting and overwhelming.

He thought his job with the 10th Mountain Division had been difficult.

"However, once she graduated college, she stopped coming around. She went to work for her mom's side of the family. When I found out Eddy left her this ranch, I will admit to being worried."

"Why?"

"I was afraid she'd changed, but she's still the same feisty little girl I remember. I believe Eddy was right in leaving the Wheeler Creek Ranch to her. She was the only choice. She's family. But I worry she can't do this alone. I'm not going to be here forever to help her and who knows what Colin and Daisy are going to do."

"Do you believe Colin and Daisy are loyal to Payton?"

"I've watched both of them grow into adults. I can't imagine that they wouldn't be. And to answer what I believe will be your next question, I don't think either would do anything to hurt her."

"So, who would? In your opinion?" Justice asked.

"Before the gray wolf was shot, I would have guessed Tim, Reemy, or James. But since they are all on the committee to save the gray wolf, I doubt they'd do that just to scare Payton off."

"That's good to know."

"Is there anything else you want to ask me? Because if not, I want to get home. My grandkids are coming to dinner tonight."

"No. That's it for now."

Topper stood. "For the record, I might not like Greg. I might have had issues with him, and I might have even been jealous of him when we were kids. However, I've never taken issue with anything that his dad has done. Eddy has been good to me. He's treated me with kindness and respect my entire career and this ranch belongs to his granddaughter. Not me." His words were spoken with conviction.

Justice stretched out his arm. He wanted to believe Topper, but he wasn't ready to bring him into the inner circle.

Yet.

Payton dropped her robe and glanced around. She hated feeling as though someone could be watching her. While she always wore her bathing suit, she still felt vulnerable. She shivered as the cold winter air smacked her exposed skin. She stepped into the hot tub, lowered herself into the bubbles to soak her muscles, and sighed.

She stared at the stars and the moon. There was nothing more soothing than a hundred and four degrees of heat on a cold night after a hard day's work, especially after the news she'd just been given. She knew she should be studying that report and dealing with it instead of trying to enjoy this simple pleasure.

But she needed time to think.

To process.

Nothing made sense.

Especially Rob's words.

The sound of the sliding glass doors caught her attention. She blinked open her eyes and turned her head. She swallowed as she stared at one hunk of a man.

"Hey. Do you mind if I join you?" Justice asked.

"Not at all." Her cheeks flushed. She tried to tell herself it was because she'd turned the temperature up all the way.

Not because she was about to be joined by one of the sexiest men she'd ever met.

Justice came outside wearing only a pair of shorts. Nothing else. Not even a pair of flip-flops.

"Aren't you freezing?"

His pecs flexed, making his tattoos shift as he climbed in. "Nope." He stretched out his arms over the sides. "The weather in the Adirondacks isn't all that much different than here. I'm used to this and honestly, I love it."

She tried to tear her gaze from the ink that lined his chest and upper arms, but she couldn't. It was a work of art and she wanted to reach out and trace the lines. The detail. She squinted, following every inch of his tattoos. She wanted to know what each one meant. Why he got it. When.

"I don't mind it most of the time," she said. "When did you get your first tattoo and which one was it?" Both of his pecs were covered in ink as well as his biceps. He had an eagle that spanned across the back of his shoulders and more tattoos along his forearms and thighs and ankles, though those were smaller. She wouldn't say he was totally covered, because there was a lot of skin left show-ing, but one could say he had an obsession with ink.

"I was sixteen," he said.

"Your parents let you when you were that young?"

He shook his head. "My buddy Wade's dad took me after he heard me trying to explain some of my scars on my chest. He decided that the lies I had made up to cover up my father beating me sucked."

Tears stung the corner of her eyes. She'd had one friend growing up who'd been abused by his father. He'd come up with some creative excuses for black eyes and broken bones. It tore her heart in two that someone as kind and caring as Justice would have to live with such pain and turmoil.

"What did your father do to you?"

"Nothing I care to repeat to a lady." He took her hand and pressed it over the dream catcher on the left side of his chest. "This was the first tattoo I got. It took five sessions to finish it."

"Because it was painful?"

He laughed. "I kind of got off on that," he said. "Compared to some of the shit my old man did, being inked was more like being tickled."

She twisted, showing off the gray wolf on her shoulder. "I don't know about that. This thing hurt like a fucker."

Fireworks exploded the second his fingers touched her skin. She swallowed, unable to move a muscle. His hand smoothed down her arm, lingering for a long few seconds before splashing into the water.

Sucking in a deep breath, she settled back into her spot and tried to act as if his touch hadn't fazed her in the least, when it would be all she would think about for the rest of the night.

"That's a beautiful tattoo."

"Thank you," she managed to croak out. It had been a long time since a man had affected her in such a way she couldn't think straight. "I've always been a big supporter of the wolf. That's why this whole shooting has me rattled. Especially on my property. My grandfather would have never allowed it. Nor would I."

"While I was checking out the ranch today after you showed me around and between interviews, I examined the scene for myself, and I don't believe the wolf was killed there."

"Rob, the wildlife agent, does. And it appears he's out for blood. Mine."

"I glanced at his report."

Payton couldn't believe what Rob had stated in his stupid little assessment of what he thought could have happened.

Gray wolf murdered with shotgun of same caliber as owner of property, who had shot her gun early that day, as stated by Payton Wheeler and confirmed by this office. It is this agent's belief that Payton Wheeler killed the alpha gray wolf, not in self-defense.

However, the report didn't have any substantial evidence. Certainly nothing to hand over to the sheriff's office to make an arrest. But that didn't mean it wouldn't make its way into the eyes of the public.

And the last thing she needed was to be judged in the eyes of the town. That could destroy her and her ranch. She wouldn't let that happen to her grandfather's legacy.

"And?" She stared at Justice who had the best resting bitch face of anyone she'd ever met.

"And nothing," he said. "The report says nothing

but an opinion based on no facts other than you shot a rifle. Big deal. That said, seven people who work for you own the same caliber weapon and they all told me they'd been shooting that day as well. Not to mention, Sheriff Sand spoke with neighbors in the area of that field. Two also own that type of weapon."

"One of them would be Hosa. He doesn't like me."

"Is that just because he's afraid of what you might do with this land? Or that you'll fail and ruin the ranch?"

"He tells people that I'm going to run my father's ranch into the ground, which will devalue his and potentially ruin his business." Payton lifted the scrunchie off her wrist and pulled her hair into a messy bun on top of her head. The contrast of the cold air clashing with the hot steam opened the pores on her face and relaxed her aching muscles. "But I've heard rumblings that he's also concerned I'll use the access road and open up lodging. He's always wanted to use his back fields to expand, but that road is on my property and we've never allowed it."

"Do you have plans to open a lodge?"

"Three years ago, my grandfather started employing show horses and cowboys for rodeos. He's got a great team. I do plan on expanding that part of the business and Topper does want me to consider possibly putting up small cabins and maybe some yurts. Where we found the gray wolf is a good spot because it's near civilization, but gives the illusion of being out in the wilderness. Daisy thinks opening a cowboy and cowgirl school is a good idea too."

"What would your grandfather have thought of those ideas?"

"I know he was down for opening up a school, especially if we could do something for kids with special needs. But opening up some kind of campground, he was on the fence. The problem is the ranch doesn't make a lot of revenue and the last three years, it's been barely turning a profit. So, it's time to make changes. The question is which ones are the right ones to pursue that aren't doing exactly what everyone is afraid of and that will change the fabric of what makes this part of the world so great. It's really a fine dance because we do need to grow with the times, but we also need to stay the same in a weird way."

"I get it," Justice said. "Lake Placid, where I grew up, has become a tourist trap. I love to go hiking there and it's so peaceful, but sometimes, the crowds are insane. Yet, we need the tourism dollars to keep things going. It's a real catch-22." He sat on the side of the hot tub, exposing his upper torso to the elements.

The steam surrounded his body like smoky

fingers curling around his muscles before disappearing as they reached for the stars and the moon shining on his glorious body.

"Aren't you cold?"

"Not yet," he said with a wicked a smile and a wink.

Every erogenous zone in her body lit up like an electrical storm. If she wasn't careful, she'd overheat. She sucked in a deep breath and let it out slowly, doing her best to squelch her desires. She wanted desperately to know what it would feel like to have his lips pressed firmly against hers and his tongue—she resisted that thought.

She narrowed her gaze and focused on the artwork on his chest. The dream catcher had such detail with fine lines and an owl in the middle. The other big tattoo was of a tiger and it was magnificent. However, she noticed raised skin underneath both.

Scars.

Reaching out with her index finger, she gently traced one of them. It was ragged, not like most scars she'd seen that had been stitched up. She stood, inching closer. "What happened?"

He took her by the wrist and tugged. He glanced down and let out a long breath. "You don't want to know."

"Yes. I do."

He brought the back of her hand to his lips and let them linger for a hot minute.

She swallowed a moan.

"You might have covered it with this ink." She palmed his chest with her other hand, running it across his body, tenderly touching other imperfections, and there were a lot of them. Some looked like scars. Others appeared to be burn marks.

All of them looked as though they'd been unattended to.

He eased back into the hot tub, pulling her down next to him, wrapping his arm around her shoulders. For a long moment, he remained silent. The only noise that filled the air was the sound of the bubbles. It tickled the inside of her ears and eased into her muscles, massaging gently. Being in his arms should feel awkward; however, she felt like she belonged. As if this was the person who was not only supposed to protect her, but perhaps there was something she needed to do for him.

She waited patiently for him to collect his thoughts. She wouldn't push—not too hard anyway—but she could tell by the way he stared at the sky that sharing was a struggle. "You won't get any judgment from me."

"I'm not worried about that."

She rested her hand on the center of his chest. "Sometimes it's good to release the past."

"I don't talk about this much," he said softly. "It

all happened a long time ago and I don't like to give my father any power over me."

"I wish I could say I understood."

"I'm glad you don't. This is not something I'd want anyone to experience."

"Are any of the scars from your time in the military?"

He tapped a few on his biceps along with what looked like bullet wounds on his gut. "These are, but I don't feel the need to cover those up."

"So, the rest are what your father did to you?"

"Yes," he said somberly, but he didn't elaborate. He continued to stare up at the sky with his lips drawn tightly together.

She wanted to press. She wanted to know. To understand. She was drawn to him in ways that didn't make sense. She barely knew him, yet she found herself feeling as though she'd known him her entire life.

That had never happened to her before.

Ever.

And then there was the undeniable passion. The desire to straddle him right there in the hot tub and find out if his kisses would be slow and tender. Or if they would be wild and out of control.

"I'm sorry," she whispered.

He ran his hand up and down her arm tenderly. "Don't be. Part of what he did to me made me a stronger man."

"I'm glad you can turn it around like that, but you were a child and he was supposed to protect you."

"That's true. But he didn't. And that's in the past."

"I can tell it still affects you."

"You're quite an intuitive person." He pressed his lips against her temple. "It's not the physical abuse that gets to me anymore. I've had to endure a lot of pain in my career. I've been shot. Stabbed. Tortured. You name it, I've dealt with it. But it's the emotional scars. The ones that are invisible. The ones that these can't cover up that still haunt me sometimes and this move to Montana has stirred it all up."

"What are you afraid of?"

He tilted her chin with his thumb and forefinger. "Someone like you."

CHAPTER 6

Justice stared into Payton's kind, caring eyes. Every time he was around her, he found himself wanting to wrap his arms around her and lose himself in her warmth. She was like no other woman he'd ever met. She was fiercely independent, yet he wanted—needed—to protect her from any and all potential threats.

This went beyond attraction. He didn't want to take her to his bed and have an enjoyable time for a few weeks. No. He desired her in ways that he didn't understand, but wanted to explore.

And that terrified him.

She jerked her head back. "What do you mean you're afraid of someone like me?"

"That didn't come out right." He tried not to laugh. That would be completely inappropriate. "My buddy, Wade, has always told me that when it comes to women, I have a tendency to open my mouth and insert both feet." He fanned his thumb across her cheek. She had to be the most naturally beautiful girl he'd ever met. He'd never seen her with a stitch of makeup on and while he was sure she could carry herself well in an evening dress and high heels, he liked her in jeans and flannel just fine.

"Sounds like you and this Wade guy are attached at the hip."

"Kind of." Justice leaned closer.

She pressed her finger over his lips.

"Oh. Sorry. I misread that situation." He recoiled. It wouldn't be the first time he'd been shot down before he'd been out of the gate. Besides, it was highly unprofessional for him to be hitting on a client. His bosses wouldn't like it. It didn't matter that occasionally some protectors ended up in long-term loving relationships, he didn't need to be the one asshole who fucked it all up.

"No. You didn't." She climbed onto his lap, wrapping her arms around his shoulders. "I just want to know what you're scared of before I let you kiss me."

He swallowed.

Hard.

He clutched at her hips, holding her steady. His vision blurred. His tongue became thick and heavy as he tried to create the words that formed in his head. "I'm not very good at this."

"At what?"

"Talking to women."

"You've been talking to me just fine since you got here." She palmed his cheek. "Are you really this shy?"

"Not sure I'd describe myself as shy. Cautious maybe. But it has more to do with trust than anything else."

Her lips parted and her eyes grew wide. "You're afraid of caring for someone because you believe they will hurt you. Or leave you."

"That's what the shrink says."

His pulse increased. Everything about her made him want to forget about all the things that frightened him when it came to relationships. She made him want to try to give a piece of himself to another human. To trust someone other than his brothers-in-arms.

"You like me," she said with a beaming smile.

"I do, but this could be a very bad idea."

"Because you work for me?" she asked in a sweet-as-honey tone.

"That's one reason." He took her mouth in a slow, but hot kiss. His tongue pushed between her lips in a search and destroy mission.

She tasted like sweet, fresh raspberries dipped in cream. A guttural moan filled his throat.

He pulled back, not wanting to let things go too far. "The other is I don't do relationships and you're the kind of person I wouldn't want to use just for sex, which is all I'm capable of."

"Bullshit," she said. "You can say that all you want, but you've already told me you're scared. It has nothing to do with your ability to be with someone for more than a moment."

"Call it what you want, but this would only be sex, and you're too good for that. You deserve someone who is all in." He wanted to bitch-slap himself. He'd been the one to start this entire thing and now he was acting like a small fucking child about it. And for what reason?

For exactly what she'd called him out on.

He was too fucking scared. But worse.

If he did take her to bed, he'd want more and that would be the end of him. He'd be lost in her and he couldn't afford to lose his heart to anyone. He had to protect the one thing he had left that made him a whole man.

"You're sweet to say that." She reached behind her back and undid her bathing suit top, letting it slip into the raging water. It swirled around, bobbing up and down, disappearing into the bubbles.

He groaned, staring at the water surrounding their bodies, which didn't cover her round breasts at all.

"I'm not asking for anything." Her fingers glided across the top of his head, through his hair, digging into his scalp. "I've never had a boyfriend long enough to think about serious relationships. I have a ranch to figure out what the future of it is going to look like. I'm also a big girl and I know exactly what this would be and I'm okay with it."

Justice searched her deep-blue eyes for a reason to remove his fingers from her tight nipples.

Her chest heaved up and down with each desperate breath.

His mind fought with this new need to be with someone he had more than sexual desire for. It was as if she reached inside him and caressed his soul. This wouldn't be about simple desires. It went deeper than that and he didn't understand how or why it happened so quickly.

"I wouldn't want to hurt you." He kissed her neck, ignoring the voice telling him to stop.

She cupped his face, tilting his head. "You have a sensitive heart. When I look in your eyes, I see a world of pain right alongside enormous compassion." She ran her hands down to the center of his chest and fanned out over his ink, fingering his scars. "This isn't like me. I don't invite men I've just met into my bedroom. I haven't done the relationship thing in a long time, but I don't do casual either."

For the first time in his life, he found someone

who understood what it was like to live in the in between, as he called it. People assumed he was commitment phobic, and he was in some ways. There were moments in his life he wished he could be different.

But then he'd never met a woman who made him want to be anything other than a man on an island.

He had his team.

His brothers.

What more did he need?

His breath hitched when his mind opened to thoughts he'd never had before. He could see him having more—a life with someone—with someone like Payton.

He took her mouth in a desperate attempt to shift his mind and body from thoughts and passions he didn't think he'd ever had to raw sex, but his heart wouldn't let him reduce her to lust. A physical need.

Wanting to savor every inch of her toned body, he lifted her from the hot tub.

She shivered and her skin rose with goose-bumps from the cold winter air. He wrapped a towel around her waist and took her hand.

"Our phones." She pointed to the small table.

"Don't want to leave those out here." He snagged both of them and tugged her toward the house. When he'd gone through her room to search for bugs, he'd admired her rustic decor. Even though the house was bigger than he could ever imagine knowing what to do with, he felt a certain peace every time he crossed the threshold.

He grew dizzy with a combination of confusion over feelings he had no idea existed and an overwhelming sense of need.

And it wasn't his own need that concerned him.

"You're beautiful," he whispered, staring into her welcoming eyes.

"You're not so bad yourself."

He felt the corners of his lips curl into a wistful smile. His heart crashed against his chest when her lips hovered over his nipple. She grazed him with her teeth.

He hissed, gritting his teeth.

She was unexpected in every way imaginable.

His breath caught in his throat as she pressed her mouth over his stomach. Her fingertips eased into his shorts, tugging at the drawstring and loosening them up.

He watched in total awe. Everything he thought he understood about who he'd become as a man had been crushed in a single kiss.

Payton had changed the center of his core. It was freeing and yet terrifying.

"Up here," he managed, gently tugging at the bun on top of her head. She smiled, licking her lips. Unable to control himself any longer, he laid her back on the bed. He nibbled on one of her puckered nipples.

Her soft moans filled his ears like waves rolling
against the rocks.

He nestled his head between her legs and she
rolled her hips against his tongue. Heat filled his
muscles.

"Yes," she said. "Please."

Running his thumb across her hard nub, he
watched the expressions on her face. Her mouth
slightly open as she bit down on her lower lip, her
eyelids fluttered open and she gasped, catching his
gaze. She jerked, clutching his wrist. Her blue orbs
widened as if in shock over the pleasure he'd
brought.

"Oh, my God," she whispered.

He licked his fingers and shifted his body. Not
wanting to put his full weight on her, he raised up
on his elbows as he slowly entered her, savoring all
the new sensations of what it felt like to be
inside her.

Her fingers dug into his back. Her chest rose
sharply. "Oh, God. Yes." She wiggled beneath him,
but he did his best to keep things as slow and
controlled as he could.

But that didn't last very long.

He thrust into her over and over again. With
each one he was rewarded with either a gasp or a
moan or the whisper of his name.

And then her body tensed before bucking wildly.

His orgasm ripped through him like raging waterfall.

An array of thick emotion squeezed at his soul.

This wasn't how it was supposed to be for him. He cared for the woman he went to bed with. He wasn't a monster like his father.

Or a cold person like his mother.

But he'd learned to keep everything locked up and protected.

Hidden away from the world so no could ever hurt him again. He would never feel abandoned. Belittled.

Or worthless again.

Because he didn't give himself completely. He saved the good stuff for himself.

He rolled to the side and pulled the covers up over their bodies, keeping one arm wrapped tightly around her while he stared at the ceiling as if it had all the answers.

Minutes ticked by as he caught his breath and his pulse returned to normal.

The fear began to creep in again.

He'd exposed himself. His heart was open to care more deeply. He wasn't sure he could put the beast back in the box.

"Are you okay?"

He kissed her temple. "I'm wonderful."

She folded her hands on his chest and rested her chin on them. "It seems like you got real distant, real quick. Like maybe you regret what happened."

"Absolutely not." That was the truth. "However, I'm not supposed to sleep with the clients." Also, kind of the truth, though three of his buddies had done just that and they still had jobs.

"I'm not going to tell anyone," she said.

He chuckled. "Neither am I, but I shouldn't sleep in here."

"Why not? No one is coming and going anymore. You won't let them," she said with a slight indignant tone. That had been a problem for a few people, but it was for everyone's safety in the end.

But that meant she was right. No one would be barging into the house unannounced.

He'd never really liked sharing a bed with anyone. He'd had a few girlfriends with whom he had to do the required spending of the night, but he struggled to sleep.

Right now, his fear was that he'd like this too much and never want to leave.

"You don't have to stay if you don't want to." She pushed from his chest and started to roll away.

"No, wait. I'm sorry." He pulled her back against his body. "I don't mean to be weird about this. But I can't become complacent in my job, which is to protect you and staying here—getting comfortable with you like this—"

"You don't have to explain yourself. It was a one-time thing. I get it."

"Sometimes I suck at this stuff." He took her chin with his thumb and forefinger. "I wouldn't mind it happening again and if the circumstances were different, I'd be all for it. I like you. You're sweet, funny, and sexy as hell. But we don't even understand what the threat is yet, so I need to be on my A game." To drive the point home, he kissed her with every ounce of desire he had filling his system.

And he was exploding with it.

"Will you do me a favor?" she asked.

"Sure."

"Will you at least stay with me until I fall asleep?"

"Of course."

She snuggled in against his chest, holding him tight. "This is much better than cuddling with a stuffed animal."

He chuckled. "You do that?"

"Every night since I was six."

"Are you saying I'm like a teddy bear?"

"Something like that."

He closed his eyes and imagined what it might be like to wake up in this room, in this very position.

It was the most glorious vision he'd ever had.

~

*D*ING.

Ding!

The sound of the motion app going off on Justice's phone startled him awake. He blinked, horrified for a brief moment, not knowing where he was or why a warm body lay sprawled out in his arms.

Payton.

Carefully, so he didn't wake her, he rolled to his side and picked up his phone.

Three in the morning.

Shit. He'd told himself he was just going to close his eyes for a moment while she dozed off and exactly what he had been afraid of—happened.

Nothing he could do about it now.

He swung his legs to the side and opened the app. A man—or at least Justice thought the height and frame could be a man—slinked around the back patio.

"Fuck." He jumped to his feet.

"What? What's happening?"

"We might have intruders."

Payton clutched the sheets to her chest for a second before she raced to the closet.

Naked.

He groaned.

This was not good.

He found his swim trunks and hiked them over his hips, securing them around his waist. "Give me that rifle." He raced around the bed.

"I'm going with you."

"Cover yourself up." He couldn't believe she was standing there with nothing on and didn't seem to notice. He snatched the rifle from her hands. It was an impressive weapon. He checked it, unlatching the safety.

She placed a handful of bullets in his palm. "I'm not sitting in this room alone."

"Fine. But seriously. You're not running around showing off that body." While she found something to wear, he checked the app. The interloper was now tiptoeing down the patio stairs. He glanced up, grateful she'd put on a shirt and shorts. "Watch my app and tell me what he's doing." He shoved the phone at her and turned. "Stay behind me and do exactly what I tell you. Got it?"

"Yes, but I'd rather have a gun in my hands."

"Mine is in my room." He didn't want to regret his actions, but he wasn't happy with them. "No time to get them and right now, I want you by my side. In the future, we'll make sure we have them with us at all times."

"Sounds like a good plan," she said. "Whoever was here is racing toward the woods."

"He's leaving?" Justice took long strides toward the sliding glass door, concerned that the shades had not been drawn. The windows had the privacy tint and made it difficult to see in, but that still didn't ease his mind.

"Looks that way and he's heading toward the trail that opens to the service road. He could have a car there."

Justice had to admit he was impressed with how calm Payton remained and how her brain shuffled through what was happening. Not many people could do that. "How close is he to the opening of the trail?" He curled his fingers around the door handle after unlocking it.

"I'd say at the pace he's running, a couple of minutes."

"That was pretty daring of anyone to come up to the house since we left the lights on outside." He pulled open the door and glanced down at a small box. "Get back. Now."

"Why?"

"Our friend left a package and Lord only knows what could be in it." During his years in the military, Justice had seen his fair share of bombs explode. It's never pretty. Not even the ones with a small amount of explosives. "Is the intruder gone?"

"I can't see him anymore."

"He could be watching us. I need you to make sure you are not in the line of fire. I want you away from any window or where a bullet could come hurling at you."

"What about you?" she asked.

"I'm doing my job." The cold hair crawled across his skin like the building of fear during a scary movie. It was slow, but it deepened, seeping right into his bones.

He shivered.

"Keep an eye on that app, though, and tell me if you see anything suspicious."

"On it."

"Shut off the outside light."

"Done," she said as it went dark.

Bending on knee, he set the rifle beside him. He glanced up, scanning the area—at least what he could see. He leaned forward, putting his ear to the box.

No sound.

That didn't mean anything.

And he didn't want to lift it in case there was some kind of trigger on the bottom.

Or there could be one on the top, though the box wasn't sealed. Just the flaps folded over.

"Should I call the police?"

"No. Not yet. I'm not sure I want them involved." While the Brotherhood Protectors worked side by side with most law enforcement agencies, he didn't know who he could trust and considering how hostile Rob, the wildlife agent, had been, he didn't know if he could trust Joe Sand, the local sheriff.

"I don't like you handling whatever that is because you're acting like it might explode."

Calling in the police would mean he'd lose some control over his protection detail. It would also bring even more attention to Payton. The headlines had not been kind. Social media was worse.

People assumed Payton had killed the wolf and they were out for blood.

This box could be a random asshole who wanted to scare her.

Or it could be something more nefarious.

"Can you see anything in the app?"

"Nothing," she said.

"Okay. I need a flashlight."

"You can use my phone." She handed it to him with the light already turned on.

Slowly, carefully, he stuck his finger under one of the flaps and shined the light. No wires. That was good. He couldn't see any metal or anything that indicated a bomb.

He tugged at the flap, holding his breath. His pulse increased, but it wasn't out of control.

The folded sides of the box opened easily and he peered inside. He exhaled a sigh of relief over the fact he wasn't going to die today.

But he didn't like the message as he stared at the words written in red on a piece of paper pinned to a decapitated stuffed animal.

You did this. If you don't leave, it might happen to you.

He lifted the box, then closed the door and locked it.

"What is it?"

"A message and not a nice one." He set the box on the small dresser opposite the bed.

"Oh, my God," she whispered. "That's Rascal."

He stared at the stuffed wolf that had its head cut off. A red bandanna was tied around the severed neck. "Is that some kind of famous wolf or something?"

"No. It's mine."

He glanced up. "How do you know?"

"Because it's not on my bed." She blinked. "I haven't been able to find it since the last time the house was cleaned."

"When exactly was that?"

"The day the gray wolf was killed," she said. "Sandy is a sweet old lady, but sometimes she doesn't put things back in the right place. I should probably let her go. She's not very good, but her husband passed six months ago and this is all she has. Monica and I are her last two clients."

"I've been meaning to talk to you about your grandfather's girlfriend, but we'll get to her in a bit," Justice said. "Did you search the house for Rascal? Did you ask Sandy about it?"

"I looked through my room, but then got

distracted and I haven't searched the rest of the house. But I know that stuffed animal in that box is mine because of the bandanna. And look on the tag." She pointed. "It has my initials on it."

Sure enough in big letters was *JW*.

"We are going to call the sheriff, but I'm going to call him directly. I don't want an entire CSI unit out here, and I don't want it on the police radio band. That will bring the media and more headlines and that could bring more of this." He pointed. "Make sure you don't touch it. My prints are on it. We don't need yours."

"Do you think whoever killed the wolf did that?"

"I honestly don't know." Justice picked up the rifle and set it next to the bed after adjusting the safety. He sat down on the edge and ran a hand across the top of his head. There was almost nothing to go by on this case and there were too many possibilities. Last he checked in with Wade, it appeared everything on the loan with Topper and his wife's business was on the up and up. She'd made some major improvements to the shop. The biggest one had been an addition to her space. All in all, Wade had stated he didn't think Topper had used the money for anything else nor that he had been in financial trouble. "It could be someone who is threatened by you or doesn't like you and saw it on the news or social media and decided to use the negative attention to scare you."

"Even with the killing of a gray wolf on my property, I wasn't overly concerned that someone was going to cause me bodily harm. It's always been that I'm an outsider. And because people do hunt the wolf, it's possible that had nothing to do with me, only now I'm thinking otherwise."

"There was no blood trail, but the wildlife doctor said the shot wouldn't have killed that creature right away." Justice knew he should have given her that piece of information sooner. It wasn't that he didn't trust her; however, he was still assessing what the goal of whoever killed the wolf had been.

Now he believed he had a better idea.

To frame her.

However, that hadn't worked. Not yet anyway.

"I hadn't thought about that." Payton climbed onto the bed, sat cross-legged, and hugged one of the pillows. "I'm officially scared."

He scooted closer and wrapped his arm around her shoulders. He wanted to promise that he'd never let anything happen to her, but he didn't believe in making declarations he couldn't be positive he could keep. He understood missions could be dangerous and things could go wrong. No matter how good he was at his job, he couldn't guarantee he could keep her from getting injured.

Or worse.

He would die trying.

"If someone wanted you dead, the bullets would be flying at you. Not at a wolf. These are meant to scare you to leave," he said. "What can you tell me about Monica Lewis? Could it be possible she wanted this ranch?"

"God, no. She's even asked me if I wanted my grandfather's antique cars back." Payton laughed. "She loved my grandfather, but she didn't love Wheeler Creek Ranch or this life. They had the strangest relationship ever. They had nothing in common. At all. Except music, whiskey, and movies."

"That sounds like a fair amount," Justice said. "So, if not Monica, let me ask you these two questions. Who would most likely step up and buy your ranch if you were to sell and who has the most to gain if you were to leave?"

"I think Hosa would want to buy it, but he doesn't have the capital. However, in some ways for him, I could be the lesser of two evils. He's been relatively nice to me in a passive-aggressive way."

"What does that mean?"

"He needs to be able to use that access road no matter what with his ATVs and we've never limited his use for that. He will take a shitty tone when talking to me and says dumb things, but he doesn't rock the boat to the point he's going to tip it over and piss us off too bad."

"But he could do something like this to get you to leave."

"I suppose." She tossed her pillow behind her and leaned back, stretching out her legs and crossing her ankles.

"I hate to ask this one because it's a bit morbid, but what about if you die? Who gets the ranch?"

"My grandfather left me a sealed note when he died and asked that I never tell anyone who I'm willing it to. He said that would cause all sorts of problems."

"Or maybe your grandfather saw this coming and didn't want someone to try to kill you." Justice arched a brow. "I think you need to show me that letter."

"I burned it."

Smart girl.

"Okay. Tell me what it said."

She held his gaze for a long moment. A sadness filled her sweet blue eyes.

He wished he could shield her from whatever pain had lifted from her soul. He'd mastered the ability to keep all his hurt just below the surface. It often found its way to his heart; however, he had tricks to push it all back down.

Only, right now, his entire childhood crashed into his gut like a bird smacking into a freshly cleaned window.

"You can trust me." His mouth went dry. His

father had told him for years he would never amount to anything. That he was useless. Worthless. That no woman would ever want him. That's why his mother left and went and raised another man's family.

His father's words stung like a fresh mosquito bite. It was as if he were a ten-year-old little boy again and his dad stood over him with a baseball bat, tapping it against his hand while reminding his only child what a loser he was and how disappointed he'd been.

Justice not only had to learn how to trust others in his life, but he also had to accept that he could be trusted and that wasn't an easy thing to do.

That feeling of failure slowly crept into his heart.

"My grandfather's words were if you tell one, that person tells one, and then you have problems."

"In order for me to protect you, I need to know."

She closed her eyes and folded her arms across her chest. "This isn't just about what my grandfather wanted. I'm telling you something no one knows. Something my grandfather has kept secret —for me."

Wow. That was a statement. "Payton. You can trust me."

"Davey," she whispered. "The ranch would go to Davey if something happened to me."

"The kid that works in the barn?" Of all the people that Justice ran through his mind, Davey was not one of them.

Topper made the most sense.

Then Colin and Daisy.

But Davey?

"Why?"

"He's my son."

CHAPTER 7

PAYTON LAY STILL on the bed, her hand firmly pressed over her flat stomach. She hadn't a single stretch mark on her belly. She'd never gotten that big. She gained all of eighteen pounds when she'd been pregnant. She'd worried it hadn't been enough. She'd been scared that while she was trying to hide the signs of her indiscretion, she was harming her unborn child. There were no physical signs she'd ever given birth.

But she remembered everything about being pregnant. Every kick of her baby. Every contraction during labor. Her child's first cry. It was loud and filled the room like a bomb going off.

She remembered the doctor telling her it was a boy. That he was small, but healthy, and then the nurse took him away without her even seeing him.

She never held her boy. Never laid eyes on him. She had no knowledge of what his eyes looked like. If they were that gray color everyone talked about, or if they had a bright-blue pigment to them, like her parents said she had.

For two days while she remained in the hospital, she mourned because she'd lost her child. He was forever gone to her.

And in a way he still was.

She was okay with that because she knew he had the best parents the universe could have given him, and she had her grandfather to thank for that. If her granddad wanted her to will the ranch to Davey, then so be it.

"Your son? How is that possible?"

"I was eighteen when I had him. No one, except me, my grandfather, and now you, knows." Her heart thumped wildly against her rib cage. Saying the words felt foreign. Almost a lie. As if she'd made up a story.

"Are you sure it's still a secret?" His warm hand rested over hers. He gently squeezed. "Could this be what all this is about? Could his family want this ranch?"

"I think they would be more afraid of me wanting to have a relationship with Davey." She blinked open her eyes. "He doesn't know he's adopted. They never told him."

"Oh." Justice rubbed the back of his neck. "No judgment, but isn't that strange?"

"It's their call. They are his parents." She believed that statement without reservation. Just because she grew that boy in her belly, that didn't make her worthy of raising him. Not at all. "I didn't know I was his mother until my grandfather told me in that letter I tossed into the fire."

"That was only six months ago," Justice whispered. "Shit. This has been a lot for you to handle."

She rolled to her side and tucked her hands under her cheek, curling her knees to her chest. "I've known that boy his entire life, but I never knew. I felt something special toward him, I think because my grandfather did, but I didn't gaze into his eyes and have some maternal feeling for him or anything."

"I hate to ask you, since I can tell this is painful, but would you please paraphrase what that note said."

A tear trickled down her face.

Justice gently wiped it away with his thumb. "I'm sorry."

"It's okay," she managed. "It's just I've never talked to anyone about this before. Not even my grandfather. After I gave birth, that was it. We never mentioned it again."

"Was that how you wanted it?"

"Yes. I wanted to forget. But I guess my grandfather didn't." She cleared her throat, gathering the strength to visualize the handwritten letter. She'd been so stunned by not only the news, but the request, that for two days, she didn't come out of the master bedroom. Everyone believed she was too grief-stricken.

Which was true.

Just not over her grandfather.

"My grandfather first apologized for having the adoption so close to home. But Charlie was desperate to give his wife a child and when this opportunity arose, he thought he could help two people he cared for. Me and Charlie. He told me to never tell anyone about the will, but begged me to do it until I had children of my own. Then I was free to leave it obviously to my family, but he did ask that I would always leave something to Davey."

"Did that ten thousand dollars that your grandfather left to the boy raise red flags?"

"Not really," Payton said. "You see, Charlie's father died working on the ranch. A bull charged him and my grandfather always felt responsible for that. So that money really is to help with the boy's education. Charlie wasn't surprised, but he also didn't want to take it. He doesn't blame my grandpa for anything."

"It sounds like your grandpa was a generous man."

"He could be to those he cared about. But if you

crossed him, he'd cut you out." Payton yawned. "I have to wonder if that's how my parents feel. I mean, it's not like they need the money. Their assets are more than what this ranch is worth, but my grandfather left me everything. And them nothing. They didn't act surprised and they didn't seem to care, but I think if my parents left me nothing, I'd be hurt."

"Have your parents ever shown any interest in this land?"

"No," she said. "At least not to me."

He pulled the covers up over her body. "Where are your parents?"

"If you're suggesting my parents would shoot a gray wolf, you're dead wrong."

"They could have hired someone."

"My parents are a lot of things, but they wouldn't do that to me. They don't like my life choice, but they support it."

Justice kissed her temple and slipped from the bed. "I have to look at every angle and I'm going to have someone check into this." He inched toward the door and carefully took the package that the intruder had left. "I'm calling the sheriff. It will take him a little bit to get out here, so sleep until then. I'll come knock on your door when he gets here."

"Promise me you won't ever tell anyone what I told you about Davey."

"I will take it to my grave."

Payton didn't trust a lot of people right now, but for whatever reason, she trusted Justice.

She closed her eyes and let her mind wander to what it had been like to have his arms wrapped around her body.

The bed felt empty.

Her heart ached for his embrace.

He'd been an unexpected complication in her life. Much like her son.

And neither one she regretted.

JUSTICE MADE TWO DECISIONS.

The first one had been not to ask Payton who the birth father had been. He'd do that today.

The second had been not to wake Payton. It wasn't necessary for her to be present while he spoke to the sheriff, especially after speaking with Stone, who stated that Joe Sand could be trusted with every aspect of this case. Even though many of his insecurities had risen to the surface, he trusted his team to a fault.

Besides, she needed a decent night's sleep. He was sure telling him about Davey had been emotionally draining. More questions could wait until she was rested and could think with a clear mind.

"What can you tell me about the wildlife agent,

Rob Altos?" Justice asked. He stood on the front porch. The temperatures were unseasonable warm for this time of year, but it was chilly. He wore his jeans, a pair of boots, and a flannel. His breath hung in the air like a ring of smoke.

"He likes to flex his muscles," Joe said. "He's passionate about his job and especially the gray wolf. He doesn't like the hunting rules."

"What about how he feels about Payton and the Wheeler Creek Ranch?"

"He's been vocal with his opinions about that." Joe leaned against the railing and folded his arms. The sun peeked out behind the mountains in the distance. The orange glow filled the sky.

Justice had always loved early mornings. When he'd been a small boy, he'd tiptoe from his room, past his father's, and out of the trailer. If he didn't get caught, he'd sit and watch the sun rise, daydreaming of the day he'd change his life.

"To be fair, no one in these parts likes outsiders. We're always worried about city folk coming in and changing the fabric of our society. We want to preserve our lifestyle and because she worked at Montgomery Development, which has destroyed some land on the East Coast, even I was on edge about her arrival." Joe held up his hand. "That said, Eddy trusted that she would do the right thing for the ranch. Eddy believed in her and the longer she keeps things the same, the more people will trust her."

"If that's the case, why all of a sudden the shift in violence? Or at least the threat of it. Everything leading up to the dead wolf and tonight has been child's play." Justice wasn't necessarily downplaying anything that had happened up to the point he'd been called in, but until tonight, things had a different tone.

Tonight had been specific.

A death threat.

And he took that personally.

His chest tightened in a way he hadn't experienced. He'd cared for women before. But not like this and he wasn't sure where to file it. His bonds with his teammates hadn't happened this quickly. Not even with Wade, who to him was like a blood brother. If he were to call anyone family, it would be Wade.

Not that his teammates weren't brothers-in-arms.

With Wade, it was different.

Wade knew his entire life story. No one else had that knowledge. His teammates had a basic understanding. A surface level awareness, but they couldn't comprehend how it controlled Justice's core. His soul.

Yet, if Payton asked, he'd willingly disclose to her everything. He tried to tell himself he could hold back; however, he knew without a doubt that his heart would want to share with her all the things that made him who he was today.

That included the darkness that lived deep inside.

"Because I'm thinking we've got two different problems here," Justice said.

"I'm inclined to agree with you." Joe shifted his gaze toward the house. "I've seen newcomers arrive all around Yellowstone and every time that happens, the locals get riled up. They do things. Dumb things like move cattle in the middle of the night from one pasture to the other. Or vandalize property. They even leave messages that have a threatening tone pinned on vehicles. But to have someone break into a home, steal a stuff animal, decapitate it, and leave a death threat after the murder of a gray wolf? Nope. That I haven't seen." Joe rubbed the back of his neck. "A couple of years ago a family moved here from Florida. They had lived a small town on a horse farm down there and knew a thing or two about that. They bought a ranch about seventy miles from here. Their neighbors did things like siphon gas from their ATVs and hide equipment. It went on for about six months and then died down when they all realized they were good people and weren't going to do anything but show horses. This is escalating and that makes me nervous."

"Who do you think has the biggest motive for wanting her gone?" Justice had categorized all the suspects, but there was one he couldn't ever say out loud.

Davey and his parents.

But it was possible there were others who knew.

Outside of them, his main suspect was Hosa, though he wasn't sure how he got into the house.

Unless he had help.

And then there was the maid, Sandy. She had access.

Monica could be a suspect, but he wasn't buying it.

The three ex-employees he'd be meeting with later. That should be interesting.

Topper didn't fit for Justice. Nor did Colin or Daisy, but he couldn't completely rule them out. He needed to spend a little more time with them to hear their story, their connections to the ranch, and how they felt about Payton.

He also needed to do some digging on her parents. The fact that this ranch skipped a generation could be an issue.

Then he needed to find out about the birth father. Perhaps he was an unknown who could want payback of some kind.

"I wanted to believe this was all a group of assholes and it would die down, but then the wolf happened. I know she didn't kill that animal. She doesn't have it in her, but I could have arrested her."

"I thought you didn't have enough evidence." Justice's heart jumped to his throat.

"It would have been a weak case and the district attorney agreed with me that it would have been too hard to prove with what we had. I was worried that he was going to run with it, but grateful he didn't. It was hard enough having to question her and treat her like a criminal."

"What's the DA's name? I'd like to talk to him."

"Phil Bradly. But be prepared for him not to take your call."

"I can be persuasive when I need to be."

"I bet you can." Joe bent over and picked up the box with the stuffed animal that he'd put in an evidence bag.

"How do you plan on keeping that private?"

"I have a few trusted people in my department," Joe said.

"The last thing we need is this getting leaked to the press."

"I will do my best." Joe gave him a slight nod. "The problem here, though, is that because of the headlines and the social media stir—which hasn't died down—this is no longer a small-town problem anymore. She's got haters everywhere and this could be more than one enemy."

"The wildlife agent isn't doing anything to help me find out who killed that gray wolf. And until that happens, I can't change that narrative and I need to." Justice felt like his brain had been cut in two, but his focus had to be on protecting Payton and that meant dealing with the threat.

Not necessarily who killed the wolf.

But they were most likely the same person.

"Call Andrea. She's a hell of a Yellowstone ranger and I know she's spending all her time looking for clues on this. She'll help you and you can trust her."

"I don't trust anyone."

"I've heard that about you," Joe said. "That's good news, bad news."

Justice laughed. "I'm well aware. But I'll give her a call."

"Good."

"I've got one more question for you before you go, and it's an odd one," Justice said.

"I'm listening."

"What can you tell me about her parents?"

"Not much about her mom. She and her family only came here to vacation. They would stay in a posh hotel and spend lots of money to pretend to enjoy the great outdoors. But I knew her dad relatively well when we were kids. We went to the same high school. I'm a grade ahead, but I knew him. He never fit in. He just didn't like it here. He always had big dreams and they didn't include being a ranch owner. When he met Roxy, he not only fell head over heels for her, but her lifestyle and family business as well."

"Montgomery Development. They build things. I've heard of them on the East Coast. They've taken small rural towns and turned them into mini cities. A lot of people don't like that," Justice said.

"Again, it doesn't make sense why people have been afraid of her, especially when Roxy's dad, before he died, wanted to own land out here and turn it into some upscale dude ranch or something. Greg has never tried to come this far west, and we all looked into it when Eddy died."

"Do you think Greg would ever do something like this to either get the land or bring his daughter back to New York?"

"Greg has always been a little underhanded, but I don't see it."

"All right. Thanks for the intel."

"My pleasure." Joe turned and headed down the steps, waving one hand over his head. "I'll be in touch."

Justice let out a long breath. He had more questions than answers. He turned and made his way back into the house. After locking the door, he strolled down the hallway. He needed a hot shower before he started his day.

He twisted the knob, turning up the heat level.

Shedding his clothes, he stepped into the massive stall. The guest shower was bigger than any bathroom he'd ever been in.

Pressing his hand against the wall, he dropped his head and let the hot water beat against his body.

He'd made so many mistakes in the last few hours and because of that, the old tapes looped in his brain.

Loser.

Worthless.

Not lovable.

If you died, no one would care.

Even in middle school, when he'd started spending the majority of his free time at Wade's house, it didn't erase the emotions that scarred his inner self. They ran so deep that no matter how hard he tried to mend them, it was as if he constantly popped a stitch, and he walked around with open wounds.

As he'd grown older, he'd learned and accepted that all those things were false. That he was a capable, intelligent human who deserved more than what he got. And he began to cover up those scars with meaningful tattoos.

But nothing could take away the damage that had been done.

It was still there. Carved deep into his soul.

If you hadn't slept with her, you would have caught the intruder.

But was that statement really true?

He would have been in his room.

Sleeping.

He wouldn't have had the second set of eyes. She helped him when it came to watching the app and looking at the box.

She might have opened the box while he was racing through the woods.

Alone.

He really needed to stop beating himself up.

All these emotions were coming from going solo. He knew this shift in careers would be hard. While they were all still working as a team, their lives were vastly different.

No one had abandoned him.

His team was still there for him and always would be.

He simply needed to carve out a place in this world that he could call his own.

The sound of the door opening caught his attention. He turned his head and wiped the aqua from his eyes. He blinked.

"You scared me," he managed, staring at a naked Payton as she stepped into the shower.

"You don't look frightened, and you didn't wake me."

He laughed, taking her into his arms. Her skin felt silky smooth under his touch. "You needed your sleep." He kissed her nose. His pulse soared.

His mind raced with contradictory thoughts. He wanted to be with her in ways he didn't understand. He trusted her and that scared him, but he feared he might let her down in some way.

It wasn't the negative voice telling him that he was unlovable either. He knew that wasn't true.

"You were so deep in thought. What were you thinking?"

"You climbed into this shower naked to ask me that?"

"Not the only reason." She leaned into him, pressing her breasts against his chest. "But I do want an answer."

He ran his hands down her back, smoothing them over her round ass. "I'll tell you after we finish in here." Kissing his way down her neck to her breasts, he sucked on her taut nipple, cupping his hand between her legs, finding her hard nub.

She gasped, gripping his shoulders.

Not wanting to give her a chance to protest, he slipped a couple of fingers inside.

He was rewarded with a throaty moan.

Every negative opinion he had of himself washed away down the drain. He'd never be able to deny her anything.

Walking away from this assignment would be harder than anything he'd ever had to do because it meant leaving Payton.

He knew this couldn't be a forever thing when

he'd started it. He didn't do things that lasted a lifetime. The relationships he had with women were because he had both physical and emotional needs. He made that clear and the women he dated didn't seem to mind.

However, none of them had been Payton and none of them had been adamant that it would end like she had.

He became frantic to be inside her. He pushed her against the shower wall, positioning himself between her legs and lifting her right off the floor. He nestled his face in her neck and groaned with the first thrust. He held himself there for a moment, catching his breath as she bit down on his shoulder.

Slowly, he repeated the motion, trying to keep his composure, but she rolled her hips not once. Not twice. But three times.

He lost all control and slammed himself into her over and over again.

"Yes. Yes," she exclaimed. "Justice."

The way his name rolled off her tongue made him crazy.

Her legs tightened around his waist. Her body shivered. "Oh, my God. Justice."

His climax came seconds after hers and caught him off guard. He braced himself against the wall. His lungs burned.

The water had turned from steamy hot to lukewarm.

He kissed her sweet lips, savoring her fruity taste. Everything he thought he wanted out of life changed. Being alone didn't seem like the perfect plan anymore.

PAYTON HANDED JUSTICE a tall mug of coffee.

"Thank you." He pushed aside the computer and adjusted his chair, facing her as she joined him at the kitchen table.

Her mind had wandered back to when she'd walked in on him in the shower. Part of her had felt as though she'd invaded his personal space. The other part had no shame in what she'd done.

And yet, there was another small part of her that was absolutely terrified for where her heart had tumbled.

The last time she fell for a man, she'd been seventeen.

He'd been twenty-one.

She wound up pregnant and he ran scared, never speaking to her again. Ever. Even when she ran into him years later, he ignored her as if they'd never met. When she'd finally cornered Sam, he'd told her that he'd moved on with his life and he hoped she had too. Of course, she knew what moving on looked like for him. He'd married a year later. He'd been all of twenty-two. He had a kid by twenty-three.

That wasn't even the problem. She was happy for him. Truly, she was.

But he never once asked how she was or what happened to their child. He simply didn't care and that spoke volumes to her about his character and the fact he had never loved her, which is what really hurt.

Since then, she protected her heart. If she was going to give it to a man, he'd have to be perfect, but that was hard to find and she hadn't been looking that hard. The ranch was her priority. If the rest didn't happen, she always thought she'd be okay.

Being around Davey gave her pause, but not enough to change her goals.

"Anyone ever tell you that you're good at avoiding conversations?" she asked.

"Yes." He lifted the mug to his lips and blew. "Marie, my buddy Wade's mom, tells me that all the time. She believes I do it when I feel vulnerable and things are getting too real."

"Is that what's happening here?" Even though Payton wanted to run, she held his gaze. She wasn't sure she really wanted to have this conversation. All she was doing was complicating her life when it came to Justice.

A relationship with him didn't seem possible.

He lived in West Yellowstone for starters.

That was almost two hours away.

Not to mention their respective careers were so different.

Why the hell was she even letting her mind go down this road?

"Because you said you'd tell me what you were thinking about in the shower and while I don't know you well, I understand you well enough to get that something was deeply troubling you and I want to know if it has to do with me. Us. My ranch and the problems I'm having. Or a combination of all of the above." She held her hands in her lap, clasping them together out of fear they'd shake.

Her muscles tensed.

She'd never been an insecure woman. Not since Sam. Once she'd managed to get over him, she'd vowed to always put herself first. She'd done that to a fault.

Sitting at her kitchen table, she wondered how she ended up with such intense feelings for a man she'd just met.

"It had more to do with me than anything else." His chest rose as he took in a deep breath. He stood. Pushing his chair in, he curled his fingers over the edge and leaned forward. "I told you my childhood was unpleasant."

"It was beyond that." She reached out and fingered the burn marks on his wrist. "There's no mistaking what these are."

"It's not the beatings that get to me. My father could take a baseball bat to me a dozen times. I know I can survive all that. It's what he did to the person." Justice tapped the center of his chest. "You know that old saying *sticks and stones may break my bones, but names will never hurt me?*"

"I do."

"For me, it's the opposite. I learned to manage the pain, but not the emotions. If it wasn't for Wade and his family—especially Marie—I probably would have turned into some angry, violent person or maybe a puddle of depression and not even be here anymore."

"Don't say that."

"But it's true," he said with great conviction. "When I was in high school, I might as well have lived at Wade's. The beatings were less and less as I got bigger and bigger. But the words, they never stopped. That was my father. The person who was supposed to love and protect me, and he failed. Miserably. But the little boy inside me sometimes believes those words." Justice turned, and walked toward the window. He folded his arms and widened his stance. "Whenever I feel like I fucked up, made a mistake, or failed at something, those memories reach up like long tentacles and echo in my mind. Marie taught me how to purge them, but it sometimes requires that I play them and that's what I was doing."

"Your dad belongs in prison." She turned her fingers into fists. She'd never heard such a horrible thing before in her entire life.

"He's been there. Twice," Justice said.

"Why didn't Wade's parents call the police?"

"I was seventeen by the time they figured it all out and I had made the decision to join the Army. I also begged them not to since another neighbor had called social services on my dad once before. It did nothing but give me a broken arm and I didn't want to risk anything happening to me being able to follow the one dream I had." He turned. His dark eyes were glazed over, but there were no tears. "Since I was fifteen, I'd wanted to join the Army. Wade wasn't going to let me do it alone, so he followed me."

"That's one hell of a friend."

"He's the best," Justice said. He sighed. "I don't know what to do about you and me. I don't feel things like this when I date."

"I'm not sure if I should take that as a compliment or not, and are we dating?"

He chuckled. "Did you know you deflect with humor when you're uncomfortable?"

"I do now." She leaned back and wrapped her arms around her middle. "What is it that you're feeling?"

"I'm not sure I can explain it. I'm not sure I want to either because now we're putting it out there in the real world, and last night we said this would only be sex."

"That is true and now we're both talking in circles."

He came back to the table and took her hand. "I want to explore what this is. I just don't know how. I'm not good at being with women."

"Um. Last night and this morning in the shower say otherwise."

He smiled. "I'm not talking about that. It's the other stuff. The intimate things that go along with a relationship. I'm told I'm cold. Unapproachable. Mean sometimes."

"How are you mean?"

He shrugged. "One lady I dated said that my communication style could be abrupt and that came across as cruel. And I'm moody."

"I'll give you moody, but never mean."

"You don't know me that well," he said. "However, I tend to not stick around very long."

"Why is that?"

"Let me answer that by first asking you a really tough question."

"Okay." She swallowed. He had this intense stare that held her hostage.

"Davey doesn't know he's adopted. If he did, or were to find out, what would your biggest fear be if he found out you're his birth mother?"

Her lips parted and a strange sound came from her voice. It vibrated in her throat. "That he would think I abandoned him and didn't love him," she whispered. She didn't have to think about the answer because it had haunted her for her entire life. But she'd been able to shove it so far into the back of her mind that she didn't have to acknowledge it for years.

Until her grandfather had died and she'd met her son and stared him in the eye.

"I know you love Davey." He palmed her cheek. "It's obvious and that's why I worry his family could be behind this, but we'll talk about that later."

"I try not to act any differently around him."

"I watched you the other morning. It's hard not to notice. And that was before I knew he was your son."

She covered her mouth.

"You didn't abandon Davey and I didn't mean to imply that you did," he said softly. "But my mother did abandon me. She left me and my dad for another man and his family. My father blamed me for it. He literally beat that concept into my psyche. When I finally found my mom, I had this idea in my head that maybe my dad was full of shit. That she'd see me and take me in, but my dad was actually telling the truth. She never wanted me. She saw me as the thing that tied her to a monster, and she left me with him and raised another man's family."

"She's as horrible as your dad." Payton shook her head. Her heart broke for the little boy—and the man—who had survived such horrors. "I'm so sorry for the life you've had to live."

"Since I left home, my life hasn't been bad," he said. "Look, since we're on this topic, I need you to understand that we need to take what happened last night as a serious death threat and that someone close to you is responsible. I have a long list of possible people, but there are three that stand out and you have to accept this is where my investigation is going, and I need your help."

"I can't imagine Charlie and Tara would do something so underhanded. They are the kind of people who would confront something head-on."

"Not if they believe their son—their family—is being threatened."

"I'm no threat," she said with a firm tone. "I would never do anything to hurt their family unit."

"But they don't know that," he said. "And that brings me to the birth father."

She recoiled, yanking her hand from Justice's warm touch. "What about him?"

"I need to know who he is."

"No." She shook her head wildly. "He's never even asked if I had the baby. For all he knows I had an abortion."

"One more reason for him to be pissed at you."

"Not that asshole," she said. "He found out I was pregnant and dumped me. He got married a year later."

"But you were only eighteen," Justice said with a scrunched face.

"He was twenty-one."

"I see. But still. I need to know who he is. Where he's living, if you know that. He's a possible suspect."

"Fine." Payton let out a long breath. "His name's Sam Hagen. Last I knew, he and his family lived in upstate New York. He's a lawyer."

"Thank you." Justice lowered his chin. "I promise to be discreet."

She believed and trusted he would do everything in his power to protect her privacy.

And her secret.

But that didn't help her unease.

"You said there were three on your main list. I take it Hosa is the other one?"

"I'm not ruling him out yet, but he's not one I'm spending today focusing on."

"Then who?"

"Your parents."

She jumped to her feet. "You've got to be

fucking kidding me. We've talked about this. There's no way. Besides, they're in New York."

"I'm having someone check into that," Justice said. "But that doesn't mean they aren't working with someone. Maybe Charlie. But we need to examine every angle and I'm not going to lie to you. I have too much respect for you."

"Well, thank you for that," she said, trying to use a sarcastic tone. She did appreciate the sentiment, but she wasn't about to let him put her parents under the microscope. Or Charlie and Tara for that matter.

Sam was an entirely different matter. He hadn't wanted anything to do with her or her pregnancy so why would he want anything to do with them now?

"However, my money is on Hosa," she said. "The more I think about it, the more he makes the most sense. He's always been so passive-aggressive with the way he deals with me. He needs that access road, but if he has an investor or if he's been talking to banks and can get a loan, he might be ready to pounce."

"We could test that theory."

"What do you mean?"

"We could put out a rumor that you're possibly looking to sell and see what pops up," Justice said.

"Oh, I wouldn't want to worry my staff that

way. They might start looking for other jobs. I can't afford to lose them."

"What if we went to him directly?"

"That might work." She nodded.

"All right. I'll get—"

Ding-dong.

"Are you expecting anyone?" Justice asked as he pulled his cell from his back pocket and tapped the screen. "Well, speak of the devil."

"Who's here?"

He held up his cell.

She leaned forward. Hosa stood on her front porch with his hands on his hips and a frown on his face.

"Let's go see what he wants."

"The only time he comes knocking on my door is to complain about something, so this should be interesting."

Justice offered his hand and she took it.

Deep down she knew he only wanted to find out who was behind the threats and to keep her safe.

She adored him for that.

Among other things.

Truly, Justice had to be the most sensitive man she'd ever met and that touched her heart, opening it up to the kind of feelings she'd thought she'd put on hold indefinitely.

CHAPTER 9

"Have a seat, Hosa." Payton waved her hand in front of the sofa.

"Thank you."

Justice planted his ass on one of the chairs across from the sofa, while Payton took the other one. She glanced between the two men, who seemed to be assessing each other.

She found that slightly amusing.

Hosa made himself comfortable on the couch. He leaned back and crossed his legs. "I'm not sure if you're aware, but an ATV came racing down the access road in the middle of the night and then had the nerve to cut through my property and right by my barn, disrupting my horses, not to mention mine and my wife's sleep."

"We didn't hear it or see it," Payton said. She sat very still, her hands draped in her lap. She did her best not to give her emotions away, something her father and Pop Pop Montgomery had taught her in the boardroom. "Or at least I didn't. Did you?" She turned her gaze toward Justice.

"I did not."

"I'm not concerned about that." Hosa tapped his cell and held it up. "It appears to be one of your ATVs at first glance. That is until you look more closely." He handed his phone to Justice.

That irked Payton. She hated being patronized by men. It happened a lot when she worked for Montgomery Development, and it continued here at Wheeler Creek Ranch.

"It has the Wheeler Creek Ranch logo on the side. It's the right color. What am I missing?" Justice asked.

"The year and model," Payton said as she took the cell. "All of mine are at least five years old. That one is brand new and it's a souped-up model. Mine are all base models." Her grandfather had been a frugal man and that had been something she hadn't been used to. She grew up being able to spend whatever whenever.

She couldn't do that anymore. She didn't have a Montgomery credit card or expense account. And while her parents would give her money if she asked for it, she wasn't about to.

"So, what you're saying is someone is posing as

someone from this ranch and racing through your property," Justice said. "But why?"

"To make it look more and more like I'm the one who set her up to take the fall for the killing of the wolf. And every other thing that has happened to her since she's rolled into town." Hosa took his phone back. "It's no secret that I've had some issues with both her and her grandfather over the access road. And I recently looked into what it would take for me to buy this ranch if Payton decided to sell."

She hated it when people spoke about her as if she wasn't in the room.

"When did you do that?" Justice asked.

"About four months ago." Hosa rested his elbows on his knees. "If Payton ever did decide to sell, I wanted to be ready. But I didn't want anyone to know because I figured most would assume I was responsible for at least some of things that happened to her and it's just not true."

"Could you please stop talking as if I'm not in the room," she said with a huff. "This is between you and me. Not you and Justice."

"I'm sorry," Hosa said. "Payton, we both know that at one time I wanted to open the access road so that I could use my west field for lodging."

"You don't want to do that anymore?" Payton asked.

"After having some professionals come out to my

property, that location is too close to my personal space. The north field is better, but I still need the access road for that. Just not between our properties."

"You want up on the other side of where the wolf was shot." Payton tilted her head. Her mind spun with the possibilities. "To come off the main route, through my land to get to yours."

"Yes." Hosa nodded. "But your grandfather was absolutely against it because of how he pushes his cattle from one parcel to the next. When you first moved here, you did the same thing, but I figured I would ask when the time was right, if you didn't sell."

"The only way I'd ever do that is if I opened my own lodging center and if you opened one right next to mine, wouldn't we be competing for the same business?"

"Not necessarily," Hosa said. "I sell out every year. I have long waiting lists. If we worked together—that is if this is something you're interested in—we wouldn't be in each other's way. I actually have a proposal I've been working on, but this honestly isn't the right moment to have that discussion."

"You're right. It's not," Justice said, leaning forward. "Why did you wait all this time to come play nice in the sandbox?"

"No offense, but she's an outsider. So are you. I wanted to make sure she wasn't going to be like her other grandfather. Montgomery Development for a good decade tried to find property out here—"

"They did not," Payton said. "I would have known." Her mother's side of the family had built cities on the East Coast. They were often misunderstood, but the reality was they did have to destroy one thing to create something else. However, it was usually for the best.

Usually.

"You weren't even born yet," Hosa said. "Or you were a baby. As a matter of fact, part of the reason your grandfather struggled with the union of his only son and Roxy Montgomery was because of who Roxy's father was and what he wanted to build in this area. When they would come to visit, your grandfather would get pissed off over Roxy and her ideas. And your dad would often side with his wife."

She knew Grandpa Wheeler had issues with Roxy. He thought she was spoiled and a bit lazy.

Not entirely false.

Her mother's love had been a bit conditional and often Payton felt smothered by both her parents. After a year into her job, she knew she'd made the wrong decision; however, she didn't believe she could simply change her mind.

"Your grandfather and I had our differences, but our families have coexisted for a hundred years and I hope we can continue to do so. I don't want to run you out of town, but I don't want to live next to something that the Montgomery's were proposing, which was essentially an all-inclusive resort for the wealthy. I offer a place for people to stay while they hike or drive off to Yellowstone. It's simple. I'm not a five-star hotel. I'm a lodge. I have cabins and yurts. Campgrounds. I attract those who want to come here to be one with nature. Not those who want to sit and sip a five-hundred-dollar bottle of wine and rent limos to take them through the park."

"That's a thing?" Justice asked.

"The Montgomery's wanted it to be a thing and frankly, it's gross." Hosa shook his head. "We need the commerce. My ranch needs the money, and no offense, Payton, but I suspect you do too; however, there are ways to do it that don't require us to sell our souls to the devil."

"I'll be honest, I've considered building campgrounds, but I wouldn't do it for a year or two. If I did, I feel like this community would have my head on a silver platter." Payton stole a quick glance toward Justice. Telling Hosa her future plans was a risk when it was possible he was behind the threats. But if he was, then things might escalate and maybe he'd trip up and they could catch him.

At least that's what she was thinking.

"They might," Hosa agreed.

"Right now, the bigger issue is where did this ATV go?"

"My ranch is the closet to town," Hosa said. "Once you get past me, you start to have homes that are larger plots until you hit the town limits. My guess is that it's either someone who lives there or someone staying close to town."

"Okay. I'll need to get a list of residents," Justice said. "And we'll need to check ATV sales."

"There's only one in this area that sells that brand," Payton said. "I know the owner. I'll give him a call."

Hosa stood. "I need to get to work. But I didn't want to let this go. I'm sorry about the things that are happening to you, especially the shooting of the gray wolf. Whoever did that is a lowlife and I hope the authorities catch them."

"Thanks." Payton stretched out her hand.

Hosa glanced at for a second before taking it in a firm shake.

She followed him to the front door and waited until he was down the steps and in his SUV before turning and facing Justice. "I actually believe him."

"So do I," Justice said. "But it makes me wonder about your parents more."

"Don't," she said. "They are wealthy people who like to build things, but they don't resort to bullying to do it. They've never had to. I worked for them for a few years. I know how they operate.

I watched them. I learned from them. If someone didn't want to sell and all the money they were willing to toss at a project didn't entice someone, they moved on. It was literally that simple. Why would they do this to me? Their own daughter? And if you bring up Davey, I'll punch you in the gut."

"I wouldn't like that," Justice said.

"Then don't do it."

"Yes, ma'am." He inched closer, curling his fingers around her biceps. "You're an amazing woman. No matter the situation, you always know how to handle yourself. I'm kind of in awe of you."

"You already got laid this morning and if you play your cards right, it could happen again tonight, so you don't have to shower me with compliments."

He kissed her cheek. "It wasn't meant to get into your pants." He patted her ass. "But now that I know it could work, I'll think of a few out-of-this-world accolades to give you."

Her stomach filled with butterflies.

She couldn't wait to hear them.

JUSTICE LEAPED from behind the steering wheel of his pickup and raced around the hood. However, he hadn't made it to the passenger side in time to be the gentleman that he wanted to be as Payton had already slipped from the seat and closed the door. "Damn, you're fast." He took her hand.

She glanced up. "Are we seriously going to walk into this dealership like a couple?"

"Oh. Sorry." He tugged his arm free. For a moment, his feelings were a little hurt. However, she had a point. He hadn't been thinking about how this would look to the outside world. What went on behind closed doors was one thing, but they didn't need to advertise.

She touched his biceps. "I don't mind. And I don't care what other people think. Only, you do."

"You're right. This is a professional call." He struggled to believe he'd gotten so relaxed in his demeanor that he forgot why they'd driven forty miles. Of course, half the trip he'd spent making flirty conversation.

Or at least he tried.

She, on the other hand, laughed at his attempts.

Which was fun in a different way.

The ways in which he felt comfortable with her stunned his core.

And yet he no longer questioned it.

He pulled open the door. "I'm not going to stop being a gentleman though. That's just the way I am."

"I could get used to someone opening doors for me." She smiled.

It sucker punched him in the gut every damn time.

He stepped into the showroom and scanned the space. It was a typical sales floor. It had five different models in the center and desks surrounding them. A few people milled about the floor, checking out various vehicles, reading the pricing sheet, or glancing at the accessories.

A woman raced from behind her desk and greeted them with a warm smile. "How can I help you?"

"My name is Payton Wheeler. Is Howard Cowell here?"

"Sure. Let me go get him." She waved her hand toward an empty desk with two chairs on one side. "Please. Have a seat over there."

"You've never met this salesperson before?" Justice asked.

"Nope. But he's on every invoice of every ATV that my grandfather bought in the last ten years."

"So, could your granddad be described as a loyal customer?"

"I'd say so," she said. "But again, no one dared do anything to piss him off because he could be a grudge holder. Which I believe is the way things are done out here."

"Why do you think he was like that?" Justice had started to paint a picture of Eddy Wheeler as a kind old man who had been hurt by his one and only son.

The question that Justice had was, did that hurt stem from disappointment? Did Eddy have expectations of Greg that Greg couldn't live up to? Had Eddy placed ridiculous demands on his only child and did those stipulations create the kind of friction that put a wedge between father and son?

Or was it simply that Greg didn't care about tradition. That he was the one who made demands on his father and gave the ultimatums.

Those kinds of dynamics were important, and Justice needed to know the nature of that relationship, outside of the eyes of Payton. He just wasn't sure where to find it. Everyone Justice spoke to at the ranch spoke about Eddy with fondness, but not so much of Greg. And when he broached the subject about their relationship, it was a mixed bag.

Some saw them as close, with the normal problems.

Others saw them as worlds apart.

Payton was a reserved woman, but she loved deeply. What struck Justice to his core was that she showed more emotion for her grandfather than she did anyone else, including her father.

But she defended her dad more than anyone else.

Perhaps that was because she shared a commonality with her father. Or what she thought was a commonality in the fact that they both made a tough decision.

Her dad left his heritage. What was rightfully his by birth because he'd fallen in love with Roxy Montgomery. A woman who happened to be the daughter of a real estate mogul from the East Coast. Greg Wheeler embraced his new world and if he did so without any consideration to his father, that could be considered a slap in the face.

"My grandfather demanded loyalty from those in his inner circle. He didn't expect everyone to bow to his every whim or anything like that. But this was his ranch. His dream. His vision. If those who worked for him didn't believe as well, they could go work somewhere else."

"Did he believe that of his son?"

"He did," Payton said. "But he didn't like it that my dad left. Or that he went to work for the Montgomerys. However, he always understood that my dad was different. He was more like my grandma."

"You don't talk about her much. What happened to her?"

Payton shifted in her seat. Her gaze shifted to her lap. "I don't really remember her."

"I'm sorry." Justice squeezed her thigh. "Did she pass away?"

"When I was seven," Payton said. "I think my father always blamed my grandpa for her death."

"May I ask how she died?"

Payton swiped at her eyes. "She was killed in a stampede of bison. It was an accident. They got spooked and there was no stopping them. Twenty people died that day."

"That's horrible." He couldn't imagine something so dreadful. "But how was your dad like her?"

"Ironically, she wasn't from Montana. She came here on vacation, met my grandfather, fell in love, and stayed. But she struggled with the lifestyle, like my dad did. That's why my grandfather let him go. That's why he didn't leave him the ranch, but left it to me. I've always felt connected to this place, but because of what happened with Davey, I walked away. I was so broken, I needed to lose myself in something else, and I guess my granddad understood that, but he always told me he wanted this place to be mine. I just thought he'd live a lot longer."

Justice wanted to tug her onto his lap and hold her tight. But that wasn't possible. Not in the middle of a showroom. Besides, a middle-aged man was headed in their direction.

"Hello," the man said. "I'm excited to finally meet you." He stretched out his arm. "I'm Howard Cowell. You must be Payton, Eddy's granddaughter."

"I am." She shook his hand. "This is my associate, Justice."

For whatever reason, he didn't like being called

by that descriptor. He wasn't sure why. It was appropriate. Completely the right term. What was she supposed to call him?

Boyfriend?

Nope.

He didn't qualify.

Or did he?

Shit.

Not the time or place for his mind to go there.

Justice nodded.

"What brings you by today?" Howard asked.

"We wanted to ask you about the latest ATV model," Justice said.

Howard squinted. "But you just bought one."

Payton exchanged a glance with Justice. "No, I didn't."

"But you did." Howard pulled open his desk drawer. "I have the paperwork. I made the sale myself. Your new ranch hand said you needed delivery that day because two of your older ones had died."

"No. All of them are running just fine and since when do you do business with anyone other than the owner?" Payton asked. "My grandfather left me details about how the business was run, and only he made these types of purchases. That hasn't changed."

"But Sam said you had made a lot of changes and he had a company credit card, though he did pay cash." Howard opened a folder and pushed it across the desk.

"Sam?" Justice questioned. "Does this man have a last name?"

"Yes. Sam Hagen."

Justice took Payton's hand and squeezed. "Are you sure?"

"Here. You can look at all the paperwork," Howard said.

"Can we get copies of all this?" Justice asked.

"I don't see why not. He made the purchase as if he were part of the ranch."

"You didn't think to question him?" Payton asked. "My grandfather always made this kind of purchase. Why wouldn't I do the same thing?"

"I'm sorry, Payton. Sam was very convincing. He drove a truck with the Wheeler Creek Ranch logo on it. He had a company credit card—"

"Did you do a credit check on that?" Justice asked.

"No. He paid cash," Howard said. "And for the record, Eddy Wheeler paid that way most of the time."

"From now on, no one buys anything here but me," Payton said.

"Understood." Howard nodded.

"Can you tell us what this man looked like?" Justice needed to redirect the discussion.

"He was young. Maybe thirtyish. Dark hair.

Long. Cowboy type. I just figured you had been making some changes since three hands had quit," Howard said.

"How did you know anyone quit?" Justice said.

"People talk." Howard closed the folder. "I'll have copies of everything made for you. I'm truly sorry for my mistake. It won't happen again."

"Thank you," Payton said.

Howard stood and headed toward the back of the showroom.

"Sam isn't thirty something, but the fact that anyone would know his name is more than disturbing," Payton said.

"Agreed." Justice took her hand. He no longer cared about appearances. "I need to know who knew about your relationship with him."

"A lot of people," she said. "Including my parents. They didn't like it because he was a few years older, but they tolerated him."

"Could your parents know about the baby?"

"I doubt it, but at this point anything is possible."

"Just go inside and put your feet up. Or take a bath." Justice placed his hand on the small of Payton's back as he nudged her toward the porch.

She wanted to dig her heels into the ground in protest. The entire drive back from town her stomach had been a ball of fire and hadn't gotten any better.

Someone knew about Sam.

That meant someone knew she had a son.

Which meant someone could know about Davey.

"I know your brain is going a mile a minute, but there isn't anything you can do but let me do my job."

"You're not helping," she said with a tight jaw. "I'm questioning everything I know about my family, and you want me to sit on my ass. I can't do that." But she didn't know what to do. There was no starting point for her. No one to call to ask questions. No rock to turn over to find answers.

"I don't want you calling them, and I certainly don't want you looking up Sam. You need to leave that to me. It's why you hired the Brotherhood Protectors."

"No. Colin made me hire you." She glared.

"I believe your name was on the check."

"That's a technicality."

He chuckled as he inserted the key to her house. "I'm going to go talk with Charlie and Tara. I've pulled Topper, Colin, and Daisy into the outer part of our circle."

"What does that mean?" She crossed the threshold and tossed her purse on the table by the split stairs and went straight for the sofa in the family, plopping herself on the soft cushions, and sighed. She focused on her tense muscles, trying to force them to relax.

But that only made it worse.

"You can talk to them about almost everything except Davey and the fact his parents are suspects."

"Oh. I guess I need to thank you for that." She had to appreciate all Justice had been doing for her, especially keeping her secret. He didn't have to do that.

"It's more than that." He sat on the edge and rested his hand on her hip, caressing gently.

His touch reached inside and eased the ache in her heart.

"They don't make sense to anyone but you and me," he said.

"Won't talking to them make everyone suspicious?"

"Davey had some great insight into people on this ranch. He's a watcher and he pays attention. I'm going to approach this interview as an apology for interrogating their son."

"That's sneaky and I don't think I like it." For fourteen years, whenever she came to the ranch and saw Davey, he was just a sweet kid who had carved a special place in her world. She found herself drawn to him and she always sought him out to spend time with him when she came to visit.

She never thought that weird because she felt the same way about Daisy.

But knowing Davey was her son changed everything and she struggled to separate the boy she had a fondness for and the son she'd given birth to.

"Because you care about him," Justice said, running his hand up and down her leg. "You want to protect him too. But I need you to trust me. Can you do that?"

"I can." She scooted to a sitting position. "Trusting you to protect me and everyone on this ranch is easy. I can see you're excellent at your job. It's the rest of it that I struggle with." She palmed his cheek. She needed Justice to understand her deepest fears. "I've told you things I've never told anyone and you hold the power to—"

"I know that's scary, and I also know that I have no clue what you went through, but part of protecting you, includes protecting Davey—"

"You believe he could be part of this." Deep down, she knew Davey could never, but she could comprehend why Justice would need to examine the boy. Just because he was a teenager didn't mean he couldn't be angry enough to lose his shit. The fact he was wickedly smart only added to that suspicion.

"Anything is possible, but for now, why don't you call Daisy to come up here and keep you company while I'm gone."

She gritted her teeth. "I don't need a babysitter."

"I know you don't, but maybe you need someone to talk to. You've spent the last six months dealing with a lot of bullshit and you've never given yourself a break. Sit in the hot tub and talk girl shit."

She laughed. "So, basically, gossip about you."

"Well, not exactly what I had in mind." He checked his watch. "I bet she's grabbing her lunch. I'm going to have a chat with Colin before I head over to see Charlie."

"How do you know the schedule?"

"I might have glanced over it a few times and

memorized it so I can know when people are coming and going," he said. "I also needed to vet Daisy. She's a good kid."

"Yeah. She is." Payton pulled out her cell. "I'll text her now."

Maybe Justice had a point. Perhaps spending an afternoon with Daisy and forgetting about the stress of everything that's going on would do her some good.

"There. Text sent." Before she had the chance to set her phone on the table, it vibrated. She glanced at the screen and smiled. "Daisy is in the bunkhouse. She'll be here in five minutes."

"Good." Justice leaned closer. "It's possible I won't be back until after dark, so don't wait up, but make sure you lock all the doors."

"Will you come join me in my room?"

"It's not a good idea," he whispered. "But most likely." He brushed his lips tenderly over her mouth. It was different from his other kisses. They were all hot and passionate, but this one was laced with thick emotion.

She clutched his shoulders, wanting to soak in all that this embrace offered.

It was like nothing she'd ever experienced.

It was as if he offered her a promise.

And she took it.

"I'll see you later," he said.

"Please text me and let me know when you're on your way."

"Of course." He stood. "Promise me you'll be safe. Keep your gun close and call me if there is anything suspicious."

"I will." She watched him stroll from the family room and down the hall. Oh boy, was she in trouble.

Since she'd been in Montana, she hadn't been involved with any man. She'd been too busy with the ranch. Before that, it had been a few months and the last man had been a bartender she'd met while out with friends in SoHo. He was fun, flirty, and so not her type.

Not that any of the men she dated were the kind of men that she thought were lifelong partner material. Those kinds of men she made sure she stayed away from. Of course, she'd been so turned off by professionals since Sam.

He'd ruined that for her when he'd been so cold and cruel.

But even a man in a suit hadn't been her idea of the perfect partner. That had been what her mom wanted for her and what her teenaged brain had been molded into believing.

Deep down, her heart always lived in Montana.

And someone like Justice was who she wanted.

No. Not someone like him.

She closed her eyes and took in a deep breath.

"Payton? Where are you?" Daisy called. "Justice let me in."

"In the family room." Payton blinked. She set her feet on the floor and adjusted her long hair. "Thanks for joining me."

"Justice informed me I have the afternoon off. Is that true?"

"It sure is and it's time for a little day drinking." Payton made her way to the bar and poured some of her favorite bourbon. "Let's go sit in the hot tub."

"I don't have a suit."

"You can borrow one of mine. Come on." Payton grabbed the liquor bottle. While she had no intention of getting shit-faced, she certainly planned on getting buzzed. Once in her bedroom, she found a couple of bathing suits and handed one to Daisy, who scrunched her nose. "What's the matter?"

"Can I ask why I'm taking the rest of the day off?"

Payton took a large gulp of her beverage. "I've had a bad day and Justice doesn't think I spend enough time with girls."

"I get he's here as a bodyguard and to help figure out who is threatening you, but is he also your boyfriend? If you don't mind me asking."

"I don't mind. But I don't know." Payton pointed to the door leading to the outside patio. "You can use the cabana bathroom. There's a robe and slippers and everything else you could possibly need. I'll see you by the spa."

Daisy's expression still hadn't changed. She looked as though she'd been forced to spend time with all the sad, pathetic girls at school for the afternoon.

As Payton changed into her bathing suit, she tried not to laugh and cry at the same time. The last thing she wanted to do was ruin Davey's life, and if he found out like this that he'd been adopted, he'd never forgive his parents.

She no longer cared about how Davey might perceive her if and when this came out. It was his relationship with the parents who raised him that mattered. Unlike Justice, who was only doing his job, she didn't believe for one minute that Charlie or his wife had anything to do with what was happening now.

That meant it could only be her parents, based on Justice's investigation.

But she didn't understand what they had to gain because she still didn't believe that Montgomery Development wanted to come this far west. They did do business in Illinois, Indiana, and Ohio, but the majority of the deals were all up and down the East Coast. They had so many projects going they had to table some opportunities and only hope they were still there when they circled back.

She finished changing into her suit and put on a

thick robe, tucking her cell into the pocket. She made her way outside with a fresh drink, but she made sure to bring the bottle.

Daisy had already climbed into the spa. She sipped her bourbon and smiled. "This is amazing. I knew it was back here, but I've never seen it."

"My grandfather put it in two years before he died and I'm not sure he used it much," Payton said as she tested the water. "I use it all the time." She hung her robe over the rack and climbed in. "Oh. God. I needed this."

"I checked the gates before I got in. They were all locked."

"Oh. Thanks. Justice would be pissed if he knew I didn't check." She eased into the hot water and let the heat work its magic on her muscles.

And all the jumbled thoughts and emotions.

When her grandfather had died, she knew the second she'd gotten the phone call she'd made a mistake by not taking the numerous job opportunities he'd given her over the years.

Every time she'd come to visit, which the older she got, became less and less, he told her she always had a place with him at the Wheeler Creek Ranch. That this was her home.

She thought she'd have more time with her grandfather, but she'd learned the hard way that life is too short.

"Speaking of Justice," Daisy said. "How is that

you don't know whether or not he's your boyfriend? I know Colin and I hooked up in an odd way since we'd known each other our entire lives and we were friends first, but from the first time we kissed, he was my boyfriend and he wouldn't dare tell anyone otherwise."

"You two make for a great couple," Payton said. "Can I ask you a question?"

"Sure, but you're avoiding my question."

Payton didn't know how to answer it so she moved on. "I've heard you're looking for property."

Daisy arched a brow. "We're looking to buy a house of our own, but not a ranch. We like our jobs here so if you're worried we're going to leave, don't be. It's just that it would be nice to have something that's ours when we get married."

"Oh. Is there a date? Did he propose?"

"No proposal. I'd hurt him. I'm not that kind of girl. We've had a discussion and we'll go down to city hall when the time is right."

"If you need a witness, I'd be happy to stand up for you. And now you have me thinking about something."

"What's that?"

"The parcel of land on the very south side of the ranch."

"The dead zone?"

Payton laughed. "It's not used for anything and while it's not on the main road, it's not far from it. It would be easy to get to work. I know it's still forty minutes to town, but that would be no different than what you're doing now."

"I don't understand what you're suggesting."

"I can't use that land for anything other than putting a building on it. However, it's not where I'd add lodging, if that's what I'd do. It's about five acres. Why not see if I can separate it from the ranch and sell it to you and Colin. You could build a nice home right there."

Daisy blinked. Five times. Slowly. Her jaw dropped open. "Are you serious?"

"Of course. And the best part is you can take your time building whatever dream home you wanted because you have a place to live now."

"I don't even know what to say. Thank you."

"You're welcome." Payton raised her glass and clanked it against Daisy's. "I'll get some numbers together and we can all sit down and discuss the details, but I do have one condition."

"I'm a little afraid to ask."

"Topper is going to retire. I will need Colin to shift to that role and you to take Colin's job."

"Oh. Well, yeah. That's not a problem."

"I'm glad to hear it."

"Now. Can we go back to the topic you're avoiding?" Daisy tilted her head back and downed the rest of her bourbon. She grabbed the bottle and poured another three fingers. "Because Justice is a tall drink of something."

"You can say that again."

"I saw him talking with Davey. Justice is not only sexy, but he's so kind and patient. He gave that boy all the attention in the world. Not everyone does that here. Seriously, Justice is a keeper."

Payton's eyes filled with tears. She turned, doing her best to hide them. "He is special." She inhaled sharply before letting it out slowly. Lifting the glass to her lips, she took three big gulps.

The brown liquid burned as it went down.

"Do you and Colin want to have children?" Payton asked.

"Someday. Maybe in five years. I'm not in a hurry."

Payton was thirty-two. She had told her parents that she wanted children in part because she wanted to shut them up. But also because deep down she did want one of her own.

One that she could keep.

At least for the first eighteen years of its life.

Parents didn't own their kids, but they were their responsibility to ensure they grew up to be good people.

Davey was a good young man. Payton believed that. She had to let Justice do his job, but she didn't think for one second that Davey could do anything to hurt anyone.

Charlie and Tara had been raising him right.

"You're young. You have plenty of time," Payton said, letting her moment pass.

"I can't do this," Daisy said. "Not when you're this emotional."

"Do what?"

"Pretend I don't know."

"What are you talking about?" Payton narrowed her stare. Her heart pounded against her rib cage so hard she thought one might crack.

"I was sixteen when I came to the ranch. You were eighteen. I know what you went through."

Payton did her best not to give her shock away. "I'm not sure what you're implying."

"You and your grandfather thought you hid your pregnancy well, but you didn't. Well, at least not from me. Or the maid, Sandy."

Payton held her breath. She didn't know what to say. If she should continue to deny. Or since the cat was already out of the bag, admit the truth.

"No one talks about it, if that makes you feel any better," Daisy said. "The only reason I know about Sandy is because I asked what happened to the baby when you came back. She told me to never breathe a word of it again. That it was none of my business. She was adamant about it. She got that weird look in her eye and waggled her finger and everything."

Payton swallowed. "I hate that look." She couldn't deny anything. "Who else knows?"

"That summer I basically had Davey's job. No one talks to you or really treats you like a ranch hand, but you get to listen to everyone. The cowboys, management, all the rodeo crew. Everyone who works on the ranch ends up asking you to do something for them and you learn a lot by closing your mouth and opening your ears."

"Sounds like my grandfather talking."

"A little bit. But I'm not sure he realized, or maybe he did, that when you do that, you learn secrets. One of the ones I learned was who knew about your pregnancy and where the baby went."

"Oh, God. No." Her worst nightmare had come true. If people knew, her parents had to know, which meant maybe Justice was right.

He needed to know what he was walking into. She reached behind her, and setting the glass on the table, she dried her hands on her robe before snagging her cell.

"I need you to tell me everyone that you're aware of who knew I was pregnant." She tripped over the last word. Her throat grew dry. She cleared it as she tapped on the screen of her phone, pulling up Justice's contact information.

"Me. Sandy. Topper and—"

"Topper knows?" If all these people knew, but never said anything, maybe her secret was still safe.

"He does. And of course, Charlie and Tara."

Crash.

Her phone dropped to the pavement.

"Shit." She leaned over. A combination of anger and humiliation filled her heart. How could all these people know and act as if nothing had ever happened? Why hadn't her grandfather warned her in his note? Did he not know?

No. He had to. He knew everything.

Which made her even more pissed that she had her head so far up her own ass that she had no idea what was right under her nose.

"Are you sure they know I'm Davey's birth mother?"

"They paid for your hospital stay."

"How do you know this?"

"Like I said. People talk around the barn girl. They don't realize it. You need to know I've never told anyone. This is not water cooler gossip."

"But if they talked about it in front of you, then maybe they did in front of Davey and he doesn't know he's adopted."

Daisy let out a big sigh and lowered her head.

Payton's pulse went from her throat to the pit of her gut. "He knows about me?"

"I don't know if has any idea who his birth mother is; however, he knows he's adopted, but as a family, they don't bring it up. And around here, it's just not something anyone talks about around you because it's what your grandfather wanted."

"This is fucking insane." She tapped Justice's name. It rang once.

"Is everything okay?" Justice asked.

"Are you at Charlie's yet?"

"I'm about to pull into his driveway. Why?"

"They've always known I'm Davey's birth mother and Davey knows he's adopted. Apparently, my grandfather is playing games from the grave for some reason."

"Well, this changes my line of questioning, as long as you're okay with it."

"I am, but please don't do anything that will hurt Davey. And he's probably not ready to know the identity of his mother yet—if ever."

"How did you find this out?"

"Daisy," Payton said. "And Topper knew. So does Sandy." She glanced up and caught Daisy's gaze. "Does Monica know?"

Daisy nodded.

"Monica knew as well."

"So, basically, your grandfather's inner circle," Justice said. "Okay. I'll be home after I finish this interview. Will you be okay until then?"

"If you call getting shit-faced okay, then yup, I'll be great."

"Is Daisy still there?" Justice asked.

"I'm here," she said loudly. "I'll stay until—"

"I don't need a babysitter," Payton said.

"If you're going to get drunk, you do, and you're not going to argue with me about it," Justice said. "I gotta go. I'll talk to you soon."

"Fucking wonderful." She set her cell on the table and sipped her drink. "I feel like an idiot."

"Did you want anyone to know about Davey?"

"I wanted to do what was best for him. That was giving him to a loving family. I was eighteen years old. I was scared and confused and I wasn't ready to be a mother."

"No one is judging you."

"Maybe not. But I feel foolish."

"Don't. I know for me I wanted to protect you and your privacy. As well as Davey and his family. I sure that's true for everyone else. Including your grandfather. If you said you didn't ever want to know, then he wanted to respect those wishes. Eddy had a big heart and he tried to make everyone happy."

Payton dropped her head back and stared at the sun as it made its way toward into the afternoon sky. Her grandfather did have a kind heart and he did do his best to make those he cared for have everything they wanted. Even his son, who abandoned ship with a woman who thought this lifestyle was beneath her. Payton's mom didn't come out and say that exactly, but she did imply it.

But so had her father.

They preferred the glitz and glamour of the Upper East Side.

Payton could understand the allure. She'd been bitten by that bug as well because she'd grown up in it.

But nothing beat living under the big Montana sky.

"Do you think Charlie and Tara are threatened by having me back?"

"I don't think so," Daisy said. "But I honestly don't know."

Well, Justice was about to find out.

CHAPTER 11

JUSTICE PULLED into Charlie's driveway just as his cell rang.

Sheriff Joe Sand.

"Hello?"

"Hi, Justice. I wanted you to know we got a hit off the prints from the box left at Payton's."

"And?" Justice placed the gearshift in park and shut down the engine.

"A guy by the name of Brent Winter. He did time for a DWI that caused bodily injury to a pedestrian back in a small town in upstate New York."

"Do you happen to know who he works for?"

"No employer listed," Joe said. "What are you thinking?"

"That Payton's father is behind this."

"That's pretty fucking sad for her if it's true."

"It sure is," Justice said. "I've got to go. For now, can you keep a lid on that?"

"I sure can."

"Also, can you send me pictures of what this guy looks like?"

"Will do," Joe said. "Watch your back."

Justice tucked his cell phone in his back pocket and headed for the front door. He rang the bell and waited about thirty seconds before Charlie opened it.

"Good afternoon," Charlie said.

"Thank you for meeting with me." Justice stretched out his hand. "Before we start, may I ask where Davey is?"

"He's at the ranch. I'm picking him up at five." Charlie guided Justice through his modest home, which was about fifteen miles from Wheeler Creek Ranch and down the road from the family restaurant, which always seemed to be busy. "Have you met my wife?" Charlie asked as they stepped into the family room.

It was decorated in a country-mountain feel with a few antlers hanging on the wall, but still had a feminine feel to it with the floral arrangements and some of the wall hangings that also had flowers.

That seemed to be a theme in the house.

"I have not," Justice said.

"I'm Tara. It's a pleasure." She gave his hand a

firm shake.

He appreciated that.

"Why did you ask where our son was?" Charlie took a seat on the sofa. His wife joined him.

Justice opted for the wooden rocking chair across from them. He organized his thoughts, choosing his words very carefully. "I wouldn't want him to overhear this conversation."

"I don't like that sound of that," Charlie said.

"I'm going to be straight with you." Justice rolled his neck. This could go really well.

Or really bad.

"Up until ten minutes ago, I had come here believing you could be behind all the threats toward Payton."

"I'm highly insulted," Charlie said. "We would never do anything to hurt that young lady."

"I thought maybe her presence might intimidate you and you'd want her gone."

Charlie and Tara shared a glance.

"Let's put all the cards on the table," Justice said. "She knows she's Davey's birth mother."

"I see," Tara said. "How long has she known?"

"Since her grandfather died," Justice said.

"Eddy told us she didn't know and that she never wanted to know where her child went. We respected those wishes," Charlie said. "She was a kid when she had Davey."

"She was so lost and scared that summer." Tara

dabbed her eyes. "It broke our hearts to see her like that. We did worry about her and that she might want to keep her baby and we always told Eddy that if in the first few months, she had second thoughts, we'd be open."

Justice swallowed.

Hard.

He really wasn't used to such caring and kind people.

Sure, Wade's parents were always willing to open their doors—and their hearts—but still. Sitting in this house, listening to Charlie and his wife, Justice began to understand what family and love was all about.

The risks.

The rewards.

"The first few times she came back, we wondered if she knew, especially when she held him," Tara said. "But she didn't. How did she find out?"

"That's not for me to tell." Justice didn't feel right giving them certain details. They would have to have that discussion with Payton.

"You said you came here because you thought we might be behind the threats? Why would we do that?" Charlie asked.

"Concern that she wanted her child back," Justice said. "Or because you were afraid she'd blow the whistle that your kid was adopted. But he already knows that. Speaking of which, do you ever worry he knows who his birth mother is, or that he'll ask?"

"We have a plan for that," Tara said.

"May I ask what that is?" Justice asked.

"First, as intuitive as he is, I don't think he knows," Tara said. "He has started to ask us how we'd feel if he wanted to find his birth mother and we told him we'd support him, which means we'd have to go to Payton."

"And we have always planned on doing that. It was a bone of contention with Eddy. He never wanted us to, but when he left Davey that money, we figured that was water under the bridge."

Justice didn't know about that based on the note, but that could have been for Payton's sake.

"We're disturbed by the things that are happening to Payton," Charlie said. "The media still hasn't died down over the gray wolf, even though there wasn't enough evidence to arrest her and I know there isn't any way she could have done it."

"I think someone is feeding the trolls on social media," a young voice said from somewhere behind Justice.

He jerked.

"Son. When and how did you get home?" Charlie was on his feet. "And why? You're not supposed to be done until five."

"Sam took me home. The new ranch hand," Davey said as if that were old news.

Justice raced to the back of the house, but whoever dropped off the kid was long gone.

Fuck.

Justice made his way back to the family room.

"Who? There's no one there by that name." Charlie stood next to his son.

"Did Sam give you a last name?" Justice asked.

"Yes. Hagen." Davey stared at him with wide eyes. "He showed me a text from my dad stating I needed to come home."

"On his phone?" Justice asked. "Did it just have your dad's name, or did it show his number?"

"His name," Davey said with a slight tremble. "Am I in trouble?"

"No, son. Not at all." Charlie wrapped his arm around the boy.

Justice pulled out his cell and tapped Payton's number. "Come on. Pick up," he mumbled.

It rang twice.

"What's up?" Payton asked.

He let out a sigh of relief.

"I don't have much time, but we have a situation. Where's Daisy?"

"Right here with me. Why?"

"Okay. Make sure all the doors are locked. I'm going to send Colin over. Don't let anyone in but him. I'll be home in twenty."

"You're scaring me. What's going on?"

"I'll explain when I get there." He tapped the phone and turned his gaze to Charlie and his boy. "Davey. Can you tell me what this Sam guy looked like?"

Davey shrugged. "He was maybe your age or a little younger. Brown hair. Dark eyes. Maybe the size of Colin."

That sounded about the same as what the salesman at the ATV dealership had described.

Justice took his cell and checked his messages.

Bingo. He had one from Joe Sand. He opened it and there was a mug shot of Brent.

"Is this him?" Justice held his phone out for Davey to examine.

"That's him," the boy nodded. "He knew a lot about the ranch. He said he'd been interviewing for a few weeks. That made sense to me because of when the others quit. He told me he came from a farm in some town in New York," Davey said with tears burning in his eyes.

Justice rested a firm hand on the boy's shoulder. "That's great detail. Thank you. I believe I at least know who is behind all this."

"I would hate for anything bad to happen to Miss Payton," Davey said.

"You and me both, kid." Justice gave him a good squeeze. "I've got to get back to the ranch. Now."

"I'm going with you," Charlie said.

"That's not—"

"If someone is about to attack, you're going to need the few hands you trust and Topper is out of town, so it's me and Colin. Besides, I'm not letting you take no for an answer." Charlie raised a brow.

"Let's go. This jerk has a good ten minutes on us," Justice said.

"I'm texting Colin now. He should be closer."

Time to catch this asshole once and for all.

PAYTON PACED in the center of her family room with her rifle in her hand. This was a far cry from the boardroom in the middle of a high-rise in Manhattan.

"You need to relax," Daisy said as she peered through the curtains.

"Right. Because you're so calm." She blew out a puff of air. "I'm sorry. I don't mean to be so sarcastic. But where the hell is Colin? He should have been here by now."

Daisy glanced at her phone. "He hasn't responded to my last text. That's not like him. Maybe I should go outside and look—"

"You are not to leave this house. Those are both Justice's and Colin's orders."

"Since when do we take orders from men?"

"Since we're not too stupid to live." Payton

rolled her shoulders. It had only been five minutes since she'd spoken to Justice. He hadn't given her much information, other than he had a name.

A New York name.

Her fucking parents.

It made no sense.

Her cell vibrated in her back pocket.

She jumped. "Fuck. That scared me." She yanked it out and stared at the incoming call. "Holy shit."

"What?" Daisy raced to her side.

"It's my dad."

"That can't be a coincidence," Daisy whispered.

Payton swallowed her breath. How could her father betray her like this? Betray his own heritage. It didn't matter that he didn't want it.

His daughter did.

She tapped the green button. "Hello, Dad," she managed, hoping her voice sounded strong. Confident.

But not cocky.

Not only did her grandfather hate that, but sometimes her parents carried that attitude. They believed it's what made them stand out in business. The first two years she worked for them, she tried it their way, and it didn't work.

The third year she realized she wasn't made for the cutthroat world of sales and her parents put her behind the scenes in Human Resources. It was a better fit for her and for them.

But even then, she wasn't fulfilled.

She missed the big sky and daydreamed of the time where she might get the courage to go ask her grandfather for a job.

Right after she told her parents she quit.

"Payton," her father said like he did when she'd been a small child and he was about to scold her.

"Is something wrong?" she asked, staring at Daisy for moral support. Her hands shook. Her heart cracked as if it had turned to stone.

This was her father and she'd been daddy's little girl her whole life.

"You couldn't just come home when things got rough," her father said. "You had to go and make your mother cry. You know I can't stand it when that happens."

"Dad. I don't have any idea what you're talking about."

The front door rattled.

Daisy snagged the rifle from her hand and aimed, but she quickly lowered it when Colin, Justice, and Charlie stepped over the threshold.

Payton's pulse calmed a tad, but not a lot. She lifted her finger to her lips. She figured her father might clam up if he knew people were listening.

"I went to a lot of trouble to drop hints about your safety there. About how you don't belong there any more than I did or your mother did, but you had to dig your heels in. You had to honor that old bastard. And your bastard child."

She covered her mouth and gasped.

He knew.

Everyone knew.

"How did you know?" she whispered.

Justice took her in his arms and guided her to the sofa. He didn't say anything, but his gentle touch spoke volumes.

"Does it matter?" her father asked.

"It does to me." She took Justice's hand and held it tight. She knew others were in the room, but she ignored them. All that mattered was this conversation with her father.

And Justice's support.

"Topper told me. He might have been loyal to your grandfather, but he didn't have a problem taking my money. Not when he needed it. Only, he got a case of the guilts or something because he's been quite loyal to your grandfather, and to you since then, and wouldn't take my money this time around."

"Is that why you had to hire an outsider?" Justice said.

"Oh. And who do I have the pleasure of speaking with?" her father asked.

"Your worst nightmare." Justice rubbed the back of his neck. "We know you sent Brent Winter here to scare Payton. We're pretty sure he's the one who killed the gray wolf."

"So what if I did," her father said. "You can't prove it and guess what?"

"I don't play games," Justice said as he held his own phone in his hand and tapped away on the screen.

"Then go open the front door and find out," her father's voice sounded sinister. She'd never heard anything like it before.

She watched in horror as Justice adjusted his weapon.

He took her by the hand and tugged her through the house. "Stay behind me," he whispered.

Holding her breath, she held on to Justice's thick arms as he yanked open the front door.

"Oh, no." She struggled to swallow the bile that smacked the back of her throat.

"Hello, daughter," her father said, holding a gun to Davey's head.

Behind him three other men were carrying machine guns.

"Aren't you happy to see me?" Her father shoved a terrified Davey into the foyer. He had his hands tied behind his back and he sported a black eye.

She cupped his face.

Charlie charged the front of the house, but her father raised a weapon.

Bang!

Charlie dropped to his knees.

"Are you fucking crazy?" Daisy raced to Charlie, ripping off her shirt and pressing it against the wound on his stomach.

Charlie groaned.

Davey cried.

Payton took him in her arms. She said nothing because no words would soothe the poor kid's heart.

"You've lost your mind," she said to her father, holding Davey close, trying to shield him from having to see his own dad sprawled out on the floor, gasping for air. "And you're not going to get away with this."

One of his goons stomped into the house and collected all the weapons. She had no idea who these people were. She'd never seen them before in her life.

"But I am. Because the person being blamed will be Sam," her father said. "When I realized I couldn't make you leave, I decided to make it look like the father of your bastard child here came after you." He reached out and rubbed the top of Davey's head.

Davey looked at her with big doe eyes. "You?" he whispered.

She blinked, taking in a long breath.

Justice's strong arm looped around her waist.

If he hadn't done that, she thought she might have fallen over.

Poor Davey, with his hands cuffed behind his back, stared at her, tears running down his cheeks. "You're my birth mother?"

"Aw, isn't this charming," her father said. "A little family reunion."

"I'm going to enjoy putting my fist in your face," Justice said.

"That's not going to happen." Her dad raised his weapon, pressing it into Justice's gut.

He groaned, but he didn't budge. "Oh. Trust me. In about ten minutes, things are going to shift in a way that you've never experienced before."

"Whatever," her father said, jerking his head. "You boys go make sure no one gets in this house." He grabbed Davey by the arm.

She tried to tug back, but her father got between them.

"Trust me when I say this will end tonight and you're not going to like the outcome. You should have gone home and made your mother happy. Now you've forced me to do things I didn't want to."

"And what's that?"

"Making sure the only person that gets this ranch is me."

CHAPTER 12

Justice knelt next to Charlie. He had some medical training as it was required of all his team members. "Let me see," he said to Daisy.

She lifted her hands.

Blood oozed from her fingers.

Shit.

Too much blood.

"Keep the pressure on." He shifted his focus, making eye contact with Charlie. "You hang tight. I've got a plan."

Charlie opened his mouth.

"Don't speak. Save your energy. You're going to need it." Justice stood and surveyed the room. One of Greg's goons stood by the door with an automatic weapon at the ready.

Greg held his ground in the center of the foyer

with his grubby hands on Davey. Payton pleaded with her father to uncuff Davey.

Colin inched closer. "I have a gun," he whispered, lifting his flannel. "So does Charlie. We're not the kind of men who leave home without them."

Payton glanced in his direction. He needed her to keep her father occupied. He gave her a head nod, hoping she'd understand.

It appeared she did because she went right back to arguing with her father. She knew the right buttons to get that man riled up. He was the type of person who had to be right and he'd keep talking until he proved his point.

And if you came back at him, he'd go again because he had to have the last word.

"I don't know who his hired hands are or what kind of training they have, but he's a moron," Justice said in a soft voice. "He'll be easy to take down. But we have to give my team some time to set up."

"Your team?" Daisy glanced up.

"My buddy Wade was fifteen minutes away doing something for me. Two of my other teammates were in the area on other assignments and the last one was driving back from—doesn't matter. They need another five minutes."

The front door rattled open and another one of Greg's musclemen walked in.

They didn't carry themselves like military men, which was good and bad. Good because that meant they weren't trained like Justice. Bad because Justice didn't know what to expect from them. But they also didn't behave like street thugs or common criminals.

"The house is secure," the man said.

"The cowboys will be coming back soon," Greg said. "The only casualties we want are those in this house. So burn everything now."

"Are you fucking kidding me?" Payton took Davey by the arm and yanked him from her father's grip, pushing him to the side and getting right in her father's face.

Oh shit.

That wasn't good.

"No. I'm not," Greg said in a calm voice.

Justice quickly reached down and found Charlie's weapon, keeping an eye on the two men with the guns, though their focus was currently on Payton. Justice tucked the weapon in his pants, covering it with his shirt.

"Why the hell would you burn down the house?" Payton asked with her hands on her hips. Her face had turned a fiery red.

Justice stood and inched closer. He had no way of contacting his team. But he wasn't worried about that. He understood how they operated. They would first figure out how many men they were dealing with outside and take them out systematically.

Gabe would most likely take the roof.

Edge and his dog would continue to deal with any threats outside.

Ridge would come in the back.

And Wade, well, he'd be the first one through the front door.

Justice's job was to be patient. Not his strong suit.

"I'm going to burn this entire fucking place down. The house. Every barn. Every inch of this nasty old place is going to burn," Greg said. "With all of you in it."

"Over my dead body," Colin said as he closed in.

Justice held out his arm, keeping Colin from doing something stupid.

"That's the point." Greg let out a long breath.

"What good would it do you to destroy the ranch? That makes it worthless," Payton said behind a tight jaw.

"It would only make ranching impossible. But I could build something on this land. Something that would draw in the most sophisticated clients. The kind of people who wouldn't think twice about dropping twenty grand on a vacation. If not more." He grabbed Payton by the shoulders. "You have a choice. You can do it with me. Or you can die in this hellhole."

A howl echoed in the night.

And then a second one.

Team wolf had arrived and was in place.

It was only a matter of minutes before they found their way inside.

"She's not dying today," Justice said. "Nor are you going to demolish this ranch."

Greg gave Justice the once-over. "I wish I could have more bullets go flying, but since that wouldn't be easily explained like an accidental fire would be, I can't shoot you."

"How are you going to deal with Charlie?" Justice needed to buy a little time. While he knew his team was out there, he didn't know if they'd found and taken out all Greg's men yet.

"You let me deal with my problems. Besides, you're a dead man, so shut up," Greg said.

Out of the corner of Justice's eye, he saw Wade dash across the hallway.

Time to make his move.

Davey had made his way to his father and sat next to Daisy.

Good.

He took Payton by the arm and tugged.

She glared.

He pleaded with his eyes, pursing his lips. "Go help Daisy with Charlie. He doesn't look good, and Davey could use your support." He turned his back and lifted his shirt. Hopefully, Wade could see he was armed.

Colin stood to his right about five feet.

"What the hell is going on?" Greg asked. His eyes shifted wildly.

Justice had no time left. He had to take out the man with the automatic weapon first. He drew his gun and aimed.

Pop!

Colin did the same as he jumped toward Greg.

Pop!

Pop!

Justice pulled the trigger again. A sharp pain sliced through his skin.

Pop! Pop! Pop!

The man holding the automatic weapon lurched back. He lifted the gun up, to the right, and then he fell backward, sliding down the door.

Wade came running into the room and immediately took down Greg.

Ridge and Edge busted through the front door and took care of the gunman.

Justice went straight for Davey. He took out his pocket knife and uncuffed the boy before turning to Payton. "Are you okay?" He glanced up just as Gabe strolled through the front door.

"The outside is secure," Gabe said.

Justice nodded.

"No. I'm not." She stared at him with wide eyes. "We need to get Charlie medical help right now."

"How long would it take to get an ambulance out here?" Justice asked.

"Too long," Daisy said. "Same for the chopper."

"But you have a helicopter," Justice said.

"The ranch pilot isn't here," Payton said.

"I'm a pilot." Justice waved Wade over. They would need to have someone attend to him inside. "What kind of medical supplies do you have here?"

"I'll go grab my kit," Payton said.

"You do that. I'll go fire up the bird." Justice let out a slow breath.

Davey grabbed his hand. "Can I go with you?"

"I'm sorry, kid. There won't be enough room for you, but I'm sure Payton can drive you." He glanced up.

She paused midstep in the hallway. She turned. "Yes. I will take you."

"Thank you," Davey said, tears streaming down his face. "Please. Make sure my dad doesn't die."

"I'll do my best." Justice nodded.

Fingers curled around his wrist.

He shifted his gaze to Charlie, who's face had turned pale. His breathing had slowed. "Fight," he said.

"I am," Charlie whispered. "But if I don't make it. Please tell my boy why we didn't tell him about

Payton. And help him understand how much she loves him."

Tears stung Justice's eyes.

"You're going to be able to tell him yourself. Now I need to go fire up that bird." Justice jumped to his feet. His adrenaline kicked into high gear again.

No one was going to die on his watch today.

PAYTON PACED in the waiting room of the hospital, biting her nail. Charlie had nearly died and it had been her fault.

It had been hours since he had come back from surgery. Davey and his mom had been called in to see him forty minutes ago.

She should leave and give them some peace, but she wanted to see Charlie.

To apologize and to guarantee she'd do whatever they asked of her as a family when it came to Davey.

She wanted them to know she understood she wasn't his mother. She gave him up and was so grateful he had the most loving family. Her grandfather had done right by all of them in that sense.

"Hey." Strong, loving arms wrapped around her body. Justice kissed her forehead. "Come sit down. You're just making yourself crazy."

"Where did all your friends go? I wanted to thank them. Especially Wade."

"They had to head back to West Yellowstone." Justice guided her toward the benches by the doors.

She rested her head on his shoulder and sighed. She wanted to ask him when he was headed back, but she was too frightened to know the answer. She closed her eyes. "Davey was so quiet on the ride here and I didn't know what to say to him."

"Things are going to be different now that he knows, and it might take him a while to accept you."

She tilted her head. "I don't want to be his mother. He has one and Tara's the best. She's a better mother than I could have ever been."

He took her by the chin with his thumb and forefinger. "Don't ever say that." He kissed her lips tenderly. "Maybe it wasn't the right time for you to be a mom and giving him up was a good thing for everyone concerned. However, someday, you're going to be a great mother."

Tears rolled freely from her eyes, dripping down her face like a waterfall. Justice was everything a woman could ever want in a man.

In a partner.

He never treated her like anything but an equal, and yet, she felt like a princess.

Something her mother—that thought made her body turn cold like a vampire. She shivered.

Justice hugged her tighter. "What's wrong?"

"I let my mind wander to my parents."

"I'm sorry that you're dealing with so much right now," Justice said. "I wish I had some great words of wisdom, but the reality is the whole thing sucks. Your father is going to spend years in prison and your mom could go as well on accessory charges."

"My phone has been blowing up. The headlines are insane."

"I wish I could make it all go away for you." He palmed her cheek and stared deep into her eyes.

She could fall head over heels in love with this man if she let herself.

And boy, did she want to.

"I had my head buried in the sand my whole life. My mom and dad were always like this. I just didn't see it."

"That's not entirely true," he said as he smoothed down her hair. "So don't beat yourself up over it."

"I should have seen it. All the signs were right in front of my face, but I did nothing, and now Charlie is in the hospital and Davey's world has been shattered."

"Listen," Justice said in such a sweet and tender voice. He was so kind and gentle. "By the time I was fifteen, I was almost six feet tall and weighed one hundred and ninety pounds. My dad might have had twenty pounds on me, but I had two inches on him. He still kicked the shit out of me and I didn't raise a fist. When I was seventeen, I was six two and two-twenty." He held up his hand. "That's when those burn marks happened."

She took his wrist and kissed every single scar.

"No matter my size, no matter how much I knew what was happening and that it was wrong, he was my dad. He was supposed to love and protect me. So, don't go playing that tape. This isn't your fault. And things with Davey will work themselves out."

"I wish I could be..."

She let her words trail off as Tara stepped through the sliding doors.

With Davey right behind her.

Payton swallowed as she pushed herself to a standing position. "How's Charlie?"

"He's asleep again. But he was telling really bad, dirty, inappropriate jokes," Tara said. "They have him on some pretty strong drugs."

"He sounds like a drunken sailor." Davey laughed, but his smile quickly faded. He stood close to his mom, clutching her forearm, almost hiding behind her as if she were protecting him from something truly terrifying.

Sometimes he looked like a big strapping young man.

Other times, like now, he appeared to be a sweet, innocent boy.

"The good news is he's going to be fine," Tara said. "They said he's going to be here for a week. Maybe less. But he's going to be out of work for a while."

"Don't worry about a thing," Payton said. "I will pay for his medical bills and continue to pay his salary."

"I appreciate that. But you know we don't need the money, and this wasn't your fault. I won't take your money," Tara said. She looped her arm around Davey and shifted her gaze. "Do you want to ask your questions?"

"Yes, ma'am." Davey nodded.

"I'll excuse myself." Justice kissed her temple. "I should probably get your helicopter back to the ranch."

"Will I see you when I get home?" she asked.

"I'll wait for you," Justice said before he turned and left.

She inhaled slowly and let it out with a big swish. "Shall we sit down?" She motioned to the one small table in the corner.

Davey pulled out a chair, sat down, and folded his hands on the surface. He picked at his thumbnail.

Something that she did when she was nervous.

Tara leaned back, resting her hand on Davey's

back. "I'm going to start by saying that some of Davey's questions might be tough for both you to answer and him to hear, but I want you to be honest. He might be young, and this situation might have happened long before any of us were ready; however, we're in it. So let's do the right thing and be open."

Payton smoothed down the front of her jeans. "I can do that."

"Thank you," Tara said. "Davey. Go ahead, honey."

"How long have you known I was your biological son?" Davey stared her square in the eye. His were glossed over, but no tears fell. He sat up tall and stiff. Anger. Confusion. Love. Fear. All those emotions poured from his body and coated her skin.

"Two weeks after my grandfather died," she said.

"You had no idea before that?" Davey asked.

She shook her head. She wanted to ask him if he'd felt something, but this moment wasn't about her and her feelings.

It was about Davey's.

"Had you planned on telling me? My parents?" Davey asked.

"Honey. I told you that Daddy and I already knew," Tara stated.

"It's okay." Payton figured the boy was going

somewhere and she had no problem being honest. "I had no intention of interfering with your life."

"So, you didn't come here to take me away from them?" Davey asked with a shaky voice. "To claim me."

"Absolutely not." She wanted to reach out and take his hand, but thought that might be too aggressive. Or too motherly. "This might be hard for you to understand, but I gave you up because I wasn't ready to be a mother. I was eighteen. I was scared. And I felt alone in this world. I begged my grandfather to find a loving family for you. Parents who would love you at least half as much as I did."

"You love me?" A single tear rolled down Davey's cheek.

Her eyes burned. She couldn't stand it another second. She reached out and took Davey's hand. "Of course I do. Loving you wasn't the problem. Being able to care for you the way a mother should was. Tara and Charlie are the best parents. Tara is your mom. Not me. I couldn't do that role well enough, but I did love you enough to give you to someone who could do it better than me. I know that's hard to understand—"

"No. I understand," Davey said. "But what I want to know is can I have both? You and my parents?"

Payton covered her mouth and swallowed a

guttural sob. "That's up to your parents," she managed.

"We want you in our lives." Tara reached across the table.

This was a lot to take in. "It's easy to say that I don't want things to change," Payton said. "Because everything's different. And I'd like for us to get to know each other better. If it's okay with your parents, maybe we can go to the movies sometime. Or go horseback riding together."

"We'd all like that," Tara said. "Thank you for giving us such a wonderful son."

Payton clutched the center of her chest. Her grandfather had done some strange things, but this one he'd gotten right.

"Charlie's brother is meeting me out front to take Davey to spend the night with his cousins," Tara said. "We need to get going. I'll keep you up to date with everything."

"Please let me know if there is anything I can do." Payton stood. "And Davey is always welcome. You know that."

"I do, but I think you should get back to that hunky Brotherhood Protector guy."

"Is Justice your boyfriend?" Davey asked. "Because he's way cool."

"He is pretty badass," Payton said. "I'm hoping he wants me to be his girlfriend because I really like him."

"Well, what are you waiting for. Go before he's sent on some other protection detail." Tara waved her hand.

Payton gave Davey a quick hug before turning and heading out the doors. She had no idea what she planned on saying to Justice.

JUSTICE LEANED against the railing on the front porch and stared at the moon and the stars. He loved the big Montana sky. It felt like a place he could call home. When his team left the military, they had stayed in the Adirondacks for a year, working search and rescue. While he had a pull to the area, he also had some horrible memories. He had a love-hate relationship with his hometown. It could be a peaceful place.

However, it could torment his soul at the same time.

Montana soothed it.

Specifically, this spot.

And then there was Payton.

She'd texted about a half hour ago and she should be arriving any minute. His pulse increased just thinking about pulling her into his arms. Holding her all night.

Waking up to her in the morning.

Damn. He had it bad.

Headlights blinded him momentarily.

Payton's pickup rolled to a stop at the base of the steps. She climbed from behind the driver's side and strolled around the hood. "Thanks for waiting."

"I had nowhere else to be right now." He smiled. "How'd your chat go?"

"Really well," she said as she jogged up the stairs. "I have a feeling that Davey's emotions are going to run hot and cold for a while, but I believe I'm prepared for that."

"Good." He opened the door for her and followed her through the foyer, down the hallway, and into the main family room where he pulled out a bottle of bourbon and poured two glasses. He handed one to her and sat on the sofa, patting the cushion.

She snuggled in next to him, curling her feet up under her cute little butt.

"Not to bring up bad things, but your mom was arrested on conspiracy charges."

"I saw that," she said. "But she'll be out by morning. I'm not sure those will stick, or at least that's what the news is saying that I listened to on the way home."

"You shouldn't be tuning into all that crap."

"I have to because it could affect my business." She took a big gulp of her drink and then set the glass on the table. She shifted, facing him dead-on.

Her blue eyes locked gazes with him in an intense stare.

His breath stuck in his lungs.

If her eyes didn't twinkle with something that could be excitement, he'd be terrified.

Though he wasn't sure exactly what emotion he should be experiencing at the moment.

"Do you have to leave tonight?"

"No." His throat was so dry he could barely speak. He downed the rest of his drink. He'd never had any intention of leaving. He'd planned on sweeping her off her feet. Romancing her, which was funny because he had no game. Right now, he couldn't think straight, much less come up with some witty line or even the courage to kiss her again.

He felt like a dumb kid on his first date.

"When do you have to get back to West Yellowstone?"

Maybe she was trying to get rid of him. Perhaps he'd misread the situation. He'd been known to do that a time or two when it came to women.

"I can be out of your hair as soon as I finish my after-action report, which can be done by dawn."

She took his glass and set it aside.

Then she straddled him. "I don't want you out of my hair."

"Oh," he said, gripping her hips. His pulse

hammered between his ears. "In that case I can email the report and ask for a few days off."

"I'd like that." She leaned in and brushed her mouth over his in a hot kiss. "I'd also like to be your girlfriend and that's the kind of thing I need to be official."

"Is it now."

"Yes." She rested her hands on his shoulders and tilted her head. "So, if you want me to rip off my clothes and race to the bedroom naked, I need to know that we're going to do our best to make a long-distance relationship work."

"Is two hours really considered long distance?" he asked. "And I get tired easily, so I might have to crash here when I come visit."

"I think a boyfriend can do that."

"Then I guess we're officially an item," he said. "My work husband is going to be jealous."

"He'll get over it."

Justice lifted her into his arms and carried her to the master. There weren't too many things in his life that made instant sense.

Wade did.

The Army did.

And now Payton.

This was where he belonged and he would do his best to make sure Payton knew he would be her equal partner.

EPILOGUE

THREE WEEKS LATER...

PAYTON LEANED against the fence and did her best not to burst out laughing. Justice might be able to ride a horse, but his ability to ride and rope left something to be desired.

However, Davey was an entirely different story. His riding skills were top notch for his age and he could certainly keep up with many of the cowboys. Charlie had mentioned that Davey wanted to get into rodeoing.

Well, he had the talent.

Payton covered her mouth as Justice rode by, his rope swinging overhead, and him nearly falling off Dumplin'.

Davey dismounted his horse and walked over. "He's getting a little better."

She smiled. "You're sweet to be spending this much time with him."

"Dad says it's helping my skills."

"Your dad is right," Payton said. "I hope your mom doesn't mind all the extra time you're spending here."

"As long as I get my chores done, and I keep getting good grades, she's okay with it." Davey took an apple and sliced it up, giving his horse a few pieces. "Miss Payton, may I ask you something?"

"Of course."

"Do you think you and Justice will get married and have kids?"

She coughed. "It's a little early to be having that conversation."

"Well, if you did, would you tell your kids that I was their brother even though I'm kind of not?"

That was quite the interesting question. "Well. First, that would be something that we'd have to sit down and discuss with your parents. But I don't see why we wouldn't. If I do have more children, I wouldn't want to lie to them about you." She looped her arm around his shoulders. "I'm not the mom who is raising you or who you call mom, but I'm still a mom."

He tilted his head and smiled. "Justice is trying so hard to impress you."

"I know." She sighed.

"You should tell him."

"Tell him what?" She stared at Davey, her heart hammering in her throat.

"That you love him because its sooooo obvious." Davey rolled his eyes.

"Maybe I'm waiting for him." She watched as Justice dismounted Dumplin' and headed their way.

"Does it matter who says it first? Because, come on, everyone knows he's head over heels for you too."

"Aren't you a kid?"

Davey laughed.

Justice rubbed the back of his neck as he approached. "I bet you two are enjoying picking on me."

"Pretty much," Davey said, taking Dumplin's reins. "I better go cool down these horses. I'll see you later." He winked.

She groaned.

"Stay out trouble, kid." Justice held out his fist.

Davey pounded it. "Always."

Justice wiped his brow before leaning in and kissing her lips. "Mmmm. You taste like sunshine."

"You're a silly man." She smiled. "Can you stay the night?"

He nodded. "But I have a briefing tomorrow

afternoon. I don't know if I can come back after that."

"I understand." And she did. His job was important. Lots of people in these parts needed protecting, especially with the increase in poaching.

He pressed his hand on the small of her back and guided her through the opening of the fence. "So, what were you and Davey talking about?"

"Interesting you should ask."

Justice laughed.

"What's so funny?"

"Was it about you and me?"

"It was, why?" she asked.

"That kid is a piece of work," Justice said.

"Hey. Watch it now. I gave birth to that boy." She climbed the steps to the front porch.

"You realize this is the spot that I first saw you," Justice said.

"Yeah. I guess so." She tilted her head. "What does that have to do with anything?"

He took her chin with his thumb and forefinger. "I'm not saying this because anyone wants me to, but the kid is right. I love you."

Her heart swelled with thick emotion. "I love you, too."

Thank you for reading *Guarding Payton*. Please feel free to leave an HONEST review!

Grab a glass of vino, kick back, relax, and let the romance roll in…

Sign up for my Newsletter (https://dl.bookfunnel.com/82gm8b9k4y) where I often give away free books before publication.

Join my private Facebook group (https://www.facebook.com/groups/191706547909047/) where I post exclusive excerpts and discuss all things murder and love!

Never miss a new release. Follow me on Amazon:amazon.com/author/jentalty

And on Bookbub: bookbub.com/authors/jen-talty

Brotherhood Protectors Yellowstone World
Team Wolf
Guarding Harper - Desiree Holt
Guarding Hannah - Delilah Devlin
Guarding Eris - Reina Torres
Guarding Payton - Jen Talty
Guarding Leah - Regan Black

INVESTIGATE WITH ME

SAIL WITH ME

FLY WITH ME

Club Temptation

SWEET TEMPTATION

The Monroes

COLOR ME YOURS

COLOR ME SMART

COLOR ME FREE

COLOR ME LUCKY

COLOR ME ICE

It's all in the Whiskey

JOHNNIE WALKER

GEORGIA MOON

JACK DANIELS

JIM BEAM

WHISKEY SOUR

WHISKEY COBBLER

WHISKEY SMASH

Search and Rescue

<u>PROTECTING AINSLEY</u>

<u>PROTECTING CLOVER</u>

<u>PROTECTING OLYMPIA</u>

<u>PROTECTING FREEDOM</u>

<u>PROTECTING PRINCESS</u>

NY STATE TROOPER SERIES

<u>*In Two Weeks*</u>

<u>*Dark Water*</u>

<u>*Deadly Secrets*</u>

<u>*Murder in paradise Bay*</u>

<u>*To Protect His own*</u>

<u>*Deadly Seduction*</u>

<u>*When A Stranger Calls*</u>

<u>*His Deadly Past*</u>

<u>*The Corkscrew Killer*</u>

Brand New Novella for the First Responders series

A spin off from the NY State Troopers series

<u>PLAYING WITH FIRE</u>

<u>PRIVATE CONVERSATION</u>

<u>THE RIGHT GROOM</u>

<u>AFTER THE FIRE</u>

<u>CAUGHT IN THE FLAMES</u>

The Men of Thief Lake

<u>REKINDLED</u>

<u>DESTINY'S DREAM</u>

Federal Investigators

<u>JANE DOE'S RETURN</u>

<u>THE BUTTERFLY MURDERS</u>

The Aegis Network

<u>THE LIGHTHOUSE</u>

<u>HER LAST HOPE</u>

<u>THE LAST FLIGHT</u>

<u>THE RETURN HOME</u>

<u>THE MATRIARCH</u>

The Collective Order

<u>THE LOST SISTER</u>

<u>THE LOST SOLDIER</u>

<u>THE LOST SOUL</u>

<u>THE LOST CONNECTION</u>

A Spin-Off Series: Witches Academy Series

<u>THE NEW ORDER</u>

Special Forces Operation Alpha

BURNING DESIRE

BURNING KISS

BURNING SKIES

BURNING LIES

BURNING HEART

BURNING BED

REMEMBER ME ALWAYS

The Brotherhood Protectors

Out of the Wild

ROUGH JUSTICE

ROUGH AROUND THE EDGES

ROUGH RIDE

ROUGH EDGE

ROUGH BEAUTY

The Brotherhood Protectors

The Saving Series

SAVING LOVE

SAVING MAGNOLIA

SAVING LEATHER

Hot Hunks

<u>**Cove's Blind Date Blows Up**</u>

<u>**My Everyday Hero – Ledger**</u>

<u>**Tempting Tavor**</u>

<u>**Needing Neor**</u>

Holiday Romances

<u>A CHRISTMAS GETAWAY</u>

<u>ALASKAN CHRISTMAS</u>

<u>WHISPERS</u>

<u>CHRISTMAS IN THE SAND</u>

<u>CHRISTMAS IN JULY</u>

Heroes & Heroines on the Field

<u>TAKING A RISK</u>

<u>TEE TIME</u>

A New Dawn

<u>**THE BLIND DATE**</u>

<u>**SPRING FLING**</u>

<u>**SUMMERS GONE**</u>

<u>**WINTER WEDDING**</u>

ABOUT JEN TALTY

Jen Talty is the *USA Today* Bestselling Author of Contemporary Romance, Romantic Suspense, and Paranormal Romance. In the fall of 2020, her short story was selected and featured in a 1001 Dark Nights Anthology.

Regardless of the genre, her goal is to take you on a ride that will leave you floating under the sun with warmth in your heart. She writes stories about broken heroes and heroines who aren't necessarily looking for romance, but in the end, they find the kind of love books are written about :).

She first started writing while carting her kids to one hockey rink after the other, averaging 170 games per year between 3 kids in 2 countries and 5 states. Her first book, IN TWO WEEKS was originally published in 2007. In 2010 she helped form a publishing company (Cool Gus Publishing) with *NY Times* Bestselling Author Bob Mayer where she ran the technical side of the business through 2016.

Jen is currently enjoying the next phase of her life…the empty nester! She and her husband reside in Jupiter, Florida.

Grab a glass of vino, kick back, relax, and let the romance roll in…

Sign up for my Newsletter (https://dl.bookfunnel.com/82gm8b9k4y) where I often give away free books before publication.

Join my private Facebook group (https://www.facebook.com/groups/191706547909047/) where I post exclusive excerpts and discuss all things murder and love!

Never miss a new release. Follow me on Amazon:amazon.com/author/jentalty

And on Bookbub: bookbub.com/authors/jen-talty

BROTHERHOOD PROTECTORS

ORIGINAL SERIES BY ELLE JAMES

Brotherhood Protectors Yellowstone

Saving Kyla (#1)

Saving Chelsea (#2)

Saving Amanda (#3)

Saving Liliana (#4)

Saving Breely (#5)

Saving Savvie (#6)

Brotherhood Protectors Colorado

SEAL Salvation (#1)

Rocky Mountain Rescue (#2)

Ranger Redemption (#3)

Tactical Takeover (#4)

Colorado Conspiracy (#5)

Rocky Mountain Madness (#6)

Free Fall (#7)

Colorado Cold Case (#8)

Fool's Folly (#9)

Brotherhood Protectors Series

Montana SEAL (#1)

Bride Protector SEAL (#2)